KRISTEN BRITAIN

SPIRIT OF
THE WOOD

A GREEN RIDER TALE

DAW BOOKS
New York

Jacket art by Donato
Jacket design by Adam Auerbach
Map and interior illustrations by Kristen Britain
Edited by Betsy Wollheim

DAW Book Collectors No. 1949

DAW Books
An imprint of Astra Publishing House
dawbooks.com
DAW Books and its logo are registered trademarks of
Astra Publishing House

Printed in the United States of America

Library of Congress Cataloging-in-Publication Data

Names: Britain, Kristen, author.
Title: Spirit of the wood : a green rider tale / Kristen Britain.
Description: First edition. | New York : DAW Books, 2023.
Identifiers: LCCN 2023033364 (print) | LCCN 2023033365 (ebook) |
  ISBN 9780756418717 (hardcover) | ISBN 9780756418724 (ebook)
Subjects: LCGFT: Fantasy fiction. | Novels.
Classification: LCC PS3552.R4964 S65 2023 (print) | LCC PS3552.R4964
  (ebook) | DDC 813/.54--dc23/eng/20230720
LC record available at https://lccn.loc.gov/2023033364
LC ebook record available at https://lccn.loc.gov/2023033365

First edition: November 2023
10 9 8 7 6 5 4 3 2 1

To Betsy Wollheim, my book mom

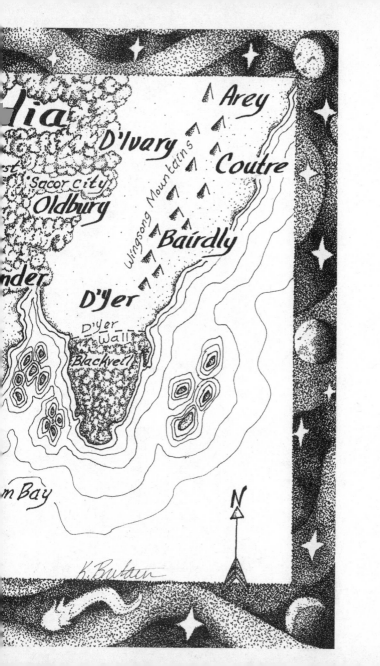

SPIRIT OF THE WOOD

THE ICE LADY

Summer was at its apex, but for all the warmth Tavin's companion exuded, it might as well have been the deep of winter. She hadn't wanted to lead a long-distance training run, and he hadn't wanted *her* to lead his.

She rode ahead of him as they made their way north. Barely a word had been spoken between them since their departure from Sacor City earlier in the month, though he'd tried to draw her out at first. His efforts had fallen flat, for her responses had consisted of one- or two-word utterances that killed any attempt at conversation. Her frosty temperament had led him to give Green Rider Lieutenant Laren Mapstone of Her Majesty's Messenger Service a nickname, at least in his own head: the Ice Lady. The other new Greenies called her worse names among themselves. They'd never do it to her face, of course, or in front of the senior Riders, especially those who'd served with her during the conflict with the Darrow Raiders, but they did so among themselves.

Goose swiped his tail at biting flies. Tavin clapped him on the neck, scattering a few more. In a matter of days they would reach the queen's royal groves within the Green Cloak

Forest. The Green Cloak was the great beating heart of Sacoridia, a dense old forest of jagged evergreen spires that blan-
keted the realm from the western provinces to as far east as
the foothills of the Wing Song Mountains. Little by little,
hardy souls were carving out homesteads for themselves to
cultivate the land, or to profit from cutting and milling tim-
ber for building ships, making paper, or any other use one
could make of wood.

Humanity's upper hand over the forest, Tavin thought,
was tenuous at best. If a farmer but glanced away from a
plot of land he'd cleared, a tangle of puckerbrush would appear. Glance away again and the next thing you knew, you
had a whole forest all grown up where once there was ara-
ble land.

Tavin had overheard enough talk among farmers who pa-
tronized his uncle's inn to know theirs was a grueling way of
life. As much as he sympathized with the plight of those who
worked the land, he had to admit he found some comfort in
the tenacity of nature.

Riding beneath the eaves of the Green Cloak, the scent
of moss and fir was heady. Squirrels chittered at them from
above. With the brooding lieutenant leading, he could almost
imagine he was by himself, and that was not such a bad thing.
In fact, it was an unexpected benefit of traveling with her.
The fortress of ice she had built around herself actually served
as a buffer between them. It contained her emotions, leaving
him largely unaffected by any spillover. He supposed he could
live with her cold demeanor if it meant not having to experience her every feeling.

As the day wore on, they encountered more travelers who mostly kept to themselves, or drovers with teams of oxen pulling sledges of logs and trailing dust. The lieutenant made no attempt to engage with them. Before leaving Sacor City, Tavin had admitted his misgivings about traveling with her to Frannie, one of the senior Riders. Frannie had told him, "Be patient. Those of us who fought the Raiders have been through a lot and seen things that will give us nightmares to the end of our days. Especially *her*. She needs this errand whether she admits it or not. She needs to get out of this castle and out of her head."

He watched her, Lieutenant Mapstone, as she rode in front, her shoulders squared, copper-red hair pulled severely back into a braid. He should be more sympathetic, he thought, to whatever she'd been through, but she didn't make it easy. The Riders mostly didn't want to talk about their experiences fighting the Darrow Raiders, but he knew enough about what those brutes had done across the realm to ordinary people, young and old, to whole villages, to have an idea of what they had seen. All the settlers in a village near his town had been tortured and butchered, and every building razed. A lot of stories like that had come through the inn. He shook his head.

A couple hours after sundown, the lieutenant called a halt for the night. Tavin was getting used to the long days in the saddle, but even with breaks, it was still hard. They took care of the horses, brushing them down and feeding them, then set up their campsite best as they could in the dark. He wished he had the special ability of night sight like Rider Nerys did. It would certainly be useful in instances like this.

His own ability had yet to manifest, and he hoped it would be a useful one.

Once they got a fire going, it made everything easier. They brewed tea, and he draped Goose's saddle blanket over a flat rock and sat on it with a deep sigh. They ate their travel rations, dried meat and hard biscuits, in silence. If it weren't so dark, he would pick blueberries from patches he'd seen along the road.

He took a sip from his waterskin and frowned at the dank tang it left on his tongue. "What I wouldn't give for a draft of old Longpond's best ale," he muttered.

The lieutenant looked up at him. "What?"

He hadn't realized he'd spoken aloud. "Oh, uh, Longpond. He's the brewer who supplies the Barefoot Bride, my uncle's inn."

"The Barefoot Bride?" She actually chuckled. "That's an unusual name for an inn. How'd that come about?"

More than a little taken aback by her interest, he replied, "Well, we're not real sure, but when my uncle bought the place, he was told the story of a bride who was so distraught by her first glimpse of her husband-to-be—it was an arranged marriage, you see—that she ran from her family's house through the snow in her bare feet and hid in the house that is now the inn. She hid there for over a year, until the marriage contract was up. Then she took her dowry and turned the place into an inn, which she ran for several years. Don't know what *she* called it, but everyone else referred to it as the barefoot bride's place, and it stuck. The story happened around seventy-five years ago, I was told."

"What happened to the bride when she finished running the inn?"

"Story goes she ran off with a handsome minstrel and was never seen in the village again, except sometimes . . ."

"Yes?"

"Well, some say her ghost can be seen, barefoot, running up the stairs in a white gown, veil over her head. Sometimes there is a presence behind the bar that isn't my uncle or one of the barkeepers. I've felt it a few times myself when I was cleaning up after closing, a cold hand on my shoulder." He shivered at the memory.

"I don't believe in ghosts," the lieutenant replied, "but it makes a good yarn. I didn't know you had worked at an inn. I take it that was in Adolind. Was it a busy place?"

"Yes, to both," he replied. A spark crackled and jumped from the fire, landing at his feet. He squashed it with the toe of his boot before it could ignite dry twigs or pine needles. "It's on a crossroad, so in addition to our locals, we got a lot of travelers, merchants, and the like."

Working there had been exhausting, not just physically, but mentally, as well, with the constant yelling and laughing of the clientele, full of wants and needs, and their waves of emotions crashing into him. It was like drowning in the undertow at times. After he was done with a shift, he'd run upstairs to his room and lock the door, and bury his head in his pillows. The pillows were insufficient at blocking out the emotions that whirled around him, but it helped some.

He took a lot of abuse from his uncle for not being friendly enough with the patrons, chatting them up, but such effort only exhausted him further. He hated it. He hated working there. The Rider call had actually been a blessing from the gods, but his fellow Riders seemed to think him reclusive when he'd decline to join them on outings to their favorite taverns. Instead, he'd grab a book and find a quiet place to read in the castle courtyard gardens, or go to the library when it was raining.

"We'll reach the waystation in a couple days," the lieutenant said. "Abram will come looking for us. You'll like him." Then she sighed. "But first we'll have to go through North."

It seemed the Ice Lady had melted a little with his tale of the Barefoot Bride, though now they fell back into their old silence. Her mention of the town of North hung heavy in the air like an ill omen.

The lieutenant settled into her bedroll. In the unguarded moment as she dropped into sleep, her walls of ice melted, unleashing raw darkness, sorrow, and despair that hit Tavin like a blow. As he sat cradling his head, he thought maybe their conversation had relaxed her tight control over her emotions. She was not an Ice Lady at all, but a fragile human barely holding herself together.

NORTH

The next day, a breeze carried shade-cooled air from the forest's deepest regions, tempering the heat that beat down on the Riders' shoulders and backs. Bees buzzed amid the small clumps of flowers growing along the road's edges, and the branches were busy with the flutterings and songs of birds. Whatever Tavin had sensed from the lieutenant the previous night had quieted, much to his relief.

They kept their pace easy. There was no urgency in their errand, and they'd reach their destination soon enough. During one of their breaks, he started relieving low-growing bushes of their blueberries. He stuffed overflowing handfuls into his mouth. Several berries rolled down his front, and sweet juice squeezed out the edges of his mouth. The lieutenant laughed as she watched him, a startling sound coming from her. She surprised him further by joining in with the picking.

Their journey continued uneventfully. Late that afternoon, just as he was feeling tired and sun baked, there was a distant roar of water and a freshening of the air. Soon he spied the glint of water between the trunks of trees. The lieutenant called a halt and turned Bluebird around to face him.

"This is the River Terrygood," she said, the lightheartedness of their blueberry feast long gone. "We're about to cross a bridge and enter the town of North. You've been informed about North in training."

It was not a question. He had been told about North all right, a rowdy town of lumberjacks, the businesses that supported the lumber trade, and those who disliked queen's law or otherwise attempted to evade it. Queen Isen had tried to post sheriffs there, but they were usually driven out. From time to time, she assigned her most disciplined troops in town—not to impose martial law, but to set up camp for a while on their way to their next post. It was an unspoken threat that if things got too out of hand, she'd force order. It wasn't all bad for North, for the mercantiles did a good business in selling to and supplying the soldiers, and the brothels received healthy custom.

"We'll not be stopping," the lieutenant said. "We'll go through at a nice easy jog. Not too slow like we're sticking around, and not too fast like we're scared witless. Do not engage if they mock us. There are a number of thugs who'd like nothing more than to provoke a fight. They know we're the queen's people, and that's enough to make them despise us."

"I understand," Tavin replied.

She was, he sensed, very calm on the surface, but a certain tension rippled outward. The muscles in his own neck were already tightening up.

"Cheer up, Rider," she said. "It may be that all is quiet today."

He hoped so. One of their fellow Riders had suffered a

head injury from a rock thrown at him in the middle of town. Luckily his horse had had the sense to carry him out even as he slumped barely conscious in the saddle.

"Ready?" she asked.

He nodded.

The hooves of Bluebird and Goose clunked and clattered on the wooden deck of the bridge as they crossed over the river. The water was flowing well, but not like it must during spring with the snowmelt.

The woods began to open up on the edge of town. Clapboard and log structures lined the road. Squat houses stood side by side with inns and taverns and brothels. Little was done to beautify the town, though one mercantile had flowers in a pot by its door.

It was pretty quiet, with few people stirring. Tavin was relieved. Everyone must be working in the woods. But then someone threw open a window and yelled, "Horse shit Greenies! Get out!" And he spat.

The lieutenant chuckled and told Tavin, "That's pretty tame by North standards."

To his mind, the Riders should be praised for the part they had played in ending the scourge of the Darrow Raiders, but then North had been left untouched, and some speculated the Raiders had found a haven here when not out murdering and raping. But even outside of North, even in Sacor City, no one lauded the Green Riders for anything, no matter their sacrifices and heroic acts.

They made it through town unscathed, and when they were about a mile out, the lieutenant halted once more and said, "Not at all bad, considering." Her relief was palpable. "It'll be a long ride, but we should be able to reach the way-station before midnight."

It would be worth the long ride to sleep with shelter over their heads for a change, Tavin thought. They clucked their horses into a sharp trot just to get some distance between them and North.

Tavin relaxed. It seemed they were free and clear of any peril North might have offered, but when they turned a bend in the road, a scene of turmoil erupted ahead. A man on a mule attempted to defend himself and his string of pack mules from three armed and mounted men.

Tavin was slammed so hard by emotions of fear and determination that he almost lost his balance and fell off Goose. A wave of consternation and surprise arose, in turn, from the attackers at the arrival of two Green Riders.

The lieutenant exclaimed to Tavin, "He's a post rider!" She drew her sword and jabbed her heels into Bluebird's sides without giving Tavin warning or further instruction. She blazed into the skirmish, her sword rising and falling as she engaged the brigands. The post rider gaped in astonishment at his savior even as he blocked a blow from one of the cutthroats with his staff.

"*Run!*" she yelled at him.

The post rider didn't hesitate. He frantically kicked his mount on, and dragged his pack mules along until they picked up into a gallop, sacks of mail bouncing on their backs. They thundered past Tavin in the direction of North.

"Aeryc and Aeryon," Tavin murmured, and realizing the

lieutenant was now beset upon by the three brigands, he grasped the hilt of his saber with a clammy hand. He'd never been in a real fight before. Heart hammering, he urged Goose forward and drew his sword to join the fray.

The lieutenant slew one of her attackers before he could pursue the post rider, and knocked the sword out of another's hand. The man, in turn, rammed his horse into Bluebird and dislodged the lieutenant from her saddle. She hit the ground hard. Before Tavin could help her, the third man engaged him.

The hard training that had been hammered into him by Arms Master Haycroft came immediately into play. Repetitive exercises in swordplay compelled him to respond to the blows without thinking. It was a good thing; otherwise, he might have frozen up.

His opponent apparently did not have the benefit of training with someone like Arms Master Haycroft and simply lashed out with his blade. Viciousness wafted off him like acrid smoke as he thrust and parried, but he left himself wide open and Tavin slashed his side. The man cried out and kicked his horse, a black-and-white piebald, into a gallop, and disappeared into the woods.

Tavin turned his attention to the lieutenant, who struggled on the ground with the man who had unhorsed her. Her attacker unsheathed a longknife. Tavin dug his heels into Goose's sides and the gelding sprang forward.

Before he could reach them, they had somehow climbed to their feet. The man cuffed the lieutenant across her face and slashed down with his knife as she stumbled backward.

Tavin scythed his saber through the neck of the brigand, nearly decapitating him. Blood sprayed as the man fell.

There was no time for Tavin to reflect on his first kill, for the lieutenant lay unmoving on her side in the dirt of the road. He threw himself off Goose and dropped to his knees beside her, rolling her onto her back.

"Dear gods," he said.

She'd been slashed from her chin down her neck, all the way to her hip bone. There was so much blood he couldn't think clearly at first, but then training took over again.

Staunch the wound, or wounds.

The menders had given the green Greenies some basic mending techniques for emergencies encountered on the road. He went to Goose and dug into his saddlebag, and pulled out shirts he'd packed for the journey. He cut and ripped them, and pressed them into the wound. It seemed deepest near her belly, but he didn't look too closely.

Her eyes fluttered open. "Did he . . ." The words came with a gasp. "Post rider. Get away?"

Intense pain flowed over Tavin. *Her* pain. He shuddered and tried to force it away. "Yes," he replied. She emanated relief. "You're hurt, Lieutenant. I've got to get you help."

"Waystation. Bluebird knows the way." Bluebird darted around them in a frenzy, issuing throaty whinnies.

"North is closer," he said. "I can get you help there."

"*No.*" The sharpness of her reply cut into him. "The waystation. Take me there. An order. The waystation . . ." Her voice faded away with her consciousness.

He shook his head. Were the people of North so barbaric

as to refuse aid to an injured queen's messenger? Would they do worse? He cursed under his breath. Whether he liked it or not, she had issued an order. He could choose to disobey it, but he could only trust in her greater experience and that she had good reason to insist that they make for the way-station.

He needed to bind her wounds so the makeshift bandages stayed put and maintained pressure to slow the flow of blood. He worried about the depth of the slash in her belly. She might bleed out before they got very far. He rolled up a blanket, and used his swordbelt and hers to fasten it to her front. This should keep the bandages in place and ensure there was some pressure on the wounds.

"I'll get you to the waystation," he told her. After that, then what? He was no mender. Where would he find help? Maybe the forester they were supposed to meet had some mending skills.

He lifted her carefully into his arms. Even the dead weight of her was not much. She was a smallish person who always seemed taller than she was. To his astonishment, Goose lay down and watched him expectantly. This made mounting, with the lieutenant in his arms, easier. After he eased into the saddle, he clucked and Goose rose to his feet. Bluebird launched into a gallop down the road, and though Goose tried to leap after him, Tavin reined him back, permitting only a gentle canter to spare the lieutenant a jostling ride. Plus, they'd be able to keep up this pace for a good while. Not so much with an all-out gallop. Bluebird reeled around on his haunches when Goose did not follow as quickly, and snorted and tossed his head in protest, but acquiesced to the canter to remain near his Rider.

Very soon they left the corpses of two brigands, and a puddle of blood soaking into the dirt where the lieutenant had lain, far behind. Tavin hoped Bluebird did, in fact, know where to go. With the lieutenant unconscious, he was assailed by only his own fear that she would die in his arms.

FLIGHT

They'd been moving along at an easy pace when shouts erupted from behind. Tavin glanced over his shoulder. A group, riding seven or eight strong, charged after him. He recognized one of the horses, the black-and-white piebald that had belonged to the brigand who'd gotten away. He'd found reinforcements.

Tavin jabbed his heels into Goose's sides. The gelding launched after Bluebird who had bolted ahead. Only as the men closed in on him did he begin to sense their eagerness for violence.

The lieutenant stirred in Tavin's arms. "What . . . ?"

"One of the cutthroats brought friends," he explained, not sure how aware of her surroundings she was.

"Bluebird. Waystation." She started to squirm.

"Please be still," he told her.

He couldn't keep balanced on Goose if she struggled. Fortunately, she subsided and drifted into unconsciousness again. Tavin peered over his shoulder and saw that his pursuers had dropped back a little. Messenger horses, with their great hearts, were hard to beat when it came to endurance and speed, but even the stoutest among them could not withstand such a pace. Plus, Goose was carrying two Riders, not one. No matter how light the lieutenant was, the additional weight would wear on him and the brigands would catch up. This, he thought, would be a good time for his special ability to emerge, a useful one, like being able to turn invisible. He'd heard there had been such an ability among the Green Riders in the past.

The woods rushed by on either side of the road. Tavin watched for some hiding place to appear that would allow him to leave the road without his pursuers being any wiser. He needed to find such an opportunity before Goose tired out. Already his neck foamed with sweat and he breathed hard. But the forest was thick, and veering off the road just now would slow him down.

The lieutenant groaned, then fell silent again. Another glance over his shoulder revealed the men falling behind some more, and then disappearing behind a bend in the road. If he could continue to increase his lead, it might be enough to allow him the time he needed to find a hiding place, or at least change mounts. Unburdened by a rider, Bluebird would be much fresher.

When he deemed the brigands far enough behind, he moderated Goose's pace again, and searched the deepening shadows for a place to hide. There were logging roads and wildlife trails, but those were too obvious. Or, maybe obvious was what he needed. On impulse, he reined Goose onto a narrow track wide enough for a sledge and pair of oxen.

The earth was churned enough that more hoofprints would not be distinguishable.

Bluebird, some lengths up the road, turned on his haunches to follow. Tavin hoped his pursuers would pass the track by, as they had all the others.

He soon directed Goose, his sides heaving from the exertion of the run, off the logging road and into the woods when he spied an outcrop. Horse hooves snapping branches and crunching on dead leaves sounded too loud to him, loud enough to be heard miles away, which was ridiculous, of course, but it was how it seemed in his heightened state of anxiety.

Once they were behind the outcrop, a granite ledge covered in moss and ferns with trees growing atop and around it, he halted. Bluebird came close to check on his Rider.

"Where . . . ?" the lieutenant asked, gazing up at Tavin.

"Shhh, we're hiding. You've got to stay quiet."

She did not seem to hear him and fussed in his arms. He tried to quiet her lest she give away their position, but it was Bluebird nuzzling her shoulder that quieted her. Tavin dared not think about how much blood she'd lost so far.

As he sat there, the distant sound of hoofbeats and voices down on the North Road drifted to him, but to his relief, the brigands continued on, not even turning down the logging road. They would not be fooled for long. He hoped it was long enough to at least give Goose and Bluebird a breather.

He carefully dismounted with the lieutenant still in his arms so he could check her wounds. There was bleed-through, but he thought the blanket-and-belts setup he had rigged had helped. He shredded another shirt to supplement her bandages before tightening the belts once more. Then he wrapped her in a blanket because she was shivering. He tried to get her to drink water, but mostly it dribbled down her chin. He made her as comfortable as he could on the ground. Since the last thing he needed was for one of the horses to go lame, he thoroughly checked them over. He then climbed to the top of the outcrop to acquire a broader view of the area.

The outcrop was not too tall, and jutted from a slight rise in the forest. At first, all was quiet in the deepening shadows as the sun began to set. There was the rustling of underbrush and leaf litter as chipmunks foraged on the forest floor. He startled at the snap of branches, but realized, with a smile, it was only a doe and her fawn. He watched them make their way, ears twitching, pausing now and then for the doe to nibble on some greenery. The fawn clung close to its mother, wagging its little tail. It was all very peaceful, he thought. He could almost forget the peril they were in.

The doe jerked her head up, and she stood stock still for several moments, watching, before she flagged the white of her tail and bounded away, her fawn close behind.

Instantly Tavin was on alert and crouched. Carefully he peered from his concealment of brush and ferns to discern what had startled the deer, but he felt the danger before he saw it—predatory intent. *Human* predatory intent.

The crack of a twig.

His heart leaped, but he remained still. Following the sound, he spotted one of the cutthroats without his horse, creeping through the forest like a hunter. The man edged along the outcrop. If he was this skilled at moving silently through the woods, he would have found sign of the passage of messenger horses. It was inevitable he would discover the lieutenant and the horses around the backside of the outcrop.

Tavin hesitated, hoping the man would simply give up and go away. He didn't want to have to confront him, because any confrontation meant that one of them would end up dead. The lieutenant moaned, however, giving away their presence.

The man paused at the sound and looked about before continuing. Tavin could sense his confidence in locating his quarry. There was no longer any possibility he would just go away. Hesitation was no longer an option. Tavin rose from his concealment, and with a running start, leaped off the outcrop, the blade of his longknife flashing in the fading light of day.

The men thudded to the ground and rolled in the leaf litter. The brigand grappled for Tavin's longknife, trying to turn it against him. The man flipped him onto his back and punched him in the face. Tavin lost hold of the knife and tasted blood.

He recovered just in time to see the knife plunging toward his chest. He grabbed the brigand's wrists and strained to hold him back, but the knife inched closer and closer. Desperate cold fear flowed through his veins and narrowed his vision to the icy steel blade.

Quite suddenly, there was a thud and the cutthroat went limp and collapsed on top of Tavin.

"Wha—?"

Tavin shoved the man off him and discovered a crater bashed into the back of his skull. Goose stood beyond, snorting and curling his lip. He dug his right front hoof, splattered with blood and viscera, into the forest loam.

After a few startled heartbeats, Tavin swallowed hard. "Thanks," he told his horse.

Tavin cut through the woods fearing that the rest of the brigands waited on the logging road. Dusk had set in, and once more he carried the lieutenant in his arms, but this time he rode Bluebird to give Goose a break.

He halted now and then to listen for the brigands, and when he heard nothing suspicious, squeezed Bluebird forward to continue picking their way through the woods. When at last they reached the North Road, he paused on the edge. He did not see or hear the presence of any humans, and what was more, he did not sense them. For now he was safe to proceed, and once Bluebird stepped onto the road, he clucked the gelding into a gentle canter.

The rush of urgent energy that had carried Tavin along after the initial fight with the brigands wore off, leaving him weary and numb. He lost track of how long he'd been riding, but the moon had risen above the trees.

He periodically walked the horses to rest them, and

switched back to riding Goose. The lieutenant was in and out of consciousness, and it took much effort to not be overcome by her confusion and pain. He hated being so sensitive to what others felt, but even as he thought it, his sensitivity saved his life, for he felt others waiting, watching, angry. The feelings came with the familiar taint of the brigands.

He had no way of knowing, however, exactly where they were, but if he could feel them, they had to be close by. Goose lifted his head looking from side to side. Tavin did not need to give a command for the horses to launch into a gallop of their own accord.

The brigands exploded from the woods and charged alongside him. They must not have expected him to pick up on their presence so soon, otherwise they could have sprung a trap from which he could not escape.

Bluebird bounded to the lead with Goose nosing up behind him. Tavin took in little detail of those who pursued him, of their weapons, or numbers. At least one of them was gone. Instead, he grimly clung to the lieutenant, giving Goose his head and trusting Bluebird to guide them.

Tavin would not win a fight. His only chance for his survival, and the lieutenant's, was the fleet-footedness of the horses.

LOGBOOK

It was a nightmare, the pounding of hooves in the dark, the shouts of the brigands. Goose stumbled and Tavin lurched in the saddle. The added weight of the lieutenant almost caused him to lose his seat and send them both tumbling over Goose's head, but Tavin held on even as Goose recovered his footing.

The stumble slowed them down long enough for one of the brigands to bump his horse into Goose's shoulder. The man grabbed Tavin's arm, but he yanked it away, and Goose surged ahead inch by inch. His breath matched Goose's; their hearts thumped in unison. He moved with the gelding's long strides, and the two became one.

The brigands fell behind, but when Bluebird suddenly plunged into the forest with Goose right behind him, Tavin could hear them following, crashing through underbrush and branches, which, as fortune would have it, further slowed them. There was a cry and Tavin glanced over his shoulder to witness a man knocked off his horse by a low-hanging limb.

Bluebird and Goose wove between the trunks of immense trees, using no discernible path, but they ran as if they'd a destination in mind. Messenger horses were smart. He'd heard a story about a mare who defended her Rider from an angry bear, and another about a messenger horse who had found the way to shelter so he and his Rider would not freeze in a blizzard. Hells, Goose had killed that man back at the outcrop, and he was very sensitive to Tavin's feelings, like when he was overwhelmed by people filling his mind with their troubles and emotions. The gelding stood faithfully by him as a solid and quiet companion.

The forest blurred by as they ran. The brigands fell behind until they were lost in the distance trying to fight their way through the tangle of the woods.

The horses slowed to a jog, and Tavin ducked to avoid a branch. A tingling across his flesh raised goosebumps. *Wards!* A small log building, tucked snug against a mossy, granite ledge, shimmered into view. All the waystations, he'd been told during training, were surrounded by wards that kept out all but Green Riders and wildlife, and apparently this forester they were supposed to meet. Bluebird had led them true.

Goose took him right up to the door and halted, then lay down again to make it easy for him to dismount with the lieutenant. She groaned with the jostling, but did not wake up. He hated to leave the care of the horses for later, exhausted and sweaty as they were, but the lieutenant, with her serious wound, needed his immediate attention. He prayed they wouldn't colic, but then to his wonder, they started walking themselves in a circle to cool off. Intelligent, indeed.

With the wards in place, the cabin required no lock, so Tavin simply pushed the door open and carried the lieutenant into the musty dark. He made out the shape of a bed with his night-adjusted sight and lay her down on the mattress. A confusing period followed in which he tried to do everything at once. He ran around lighting candles and flinging open shutters and windows to let fresh air in, and searched for helpful supplies, while pausing frequently to ensure the lieutenant was still breathing.

The Riders kept the waystations supplied. Every year, small teams went out to each of the stations with everything from fresh uniform parts to fodder for the horses to place in storage for any Riders passing through and in need. He yanked open a closet door, and the pleasant scent of cedar wafted into the air. Inside were uniforms, bedclothes, and pillows, and sitting at the bottom on the floor, a small chest. He hauled it out and threw the lid open. There! Emergency mending supplies.

He grabbed bandages and a bottle of whiskey, then realized he needed water. The station would not have been built here without a ready source of water.

"I'll be right back," he told the lieutenant, though he was uncertain if she was capable of hearing anything in her unconscious state.

He found a cold, clear spring bubbling in the moonlight behind the cabin, and filled a pitcher. Bluebird paced around him, snorting and whinnying. Tavin was glad the emotions of horses did not bleed as strongly into him as those of people.

"I'm looking after her," he said, "but I need the water to clean her wounds."

Bluebird left him alone then. When Tavin returned inside, he found the lieutenant writhing on the bed and moaning. She tugged at the belts that fastened the blanket and bandages to her wound.

"Stop now," he told her, setting the pitcher aside. He gently grabbed her hands. "Stop now or you'll make it worse."

She was too weak to fight him, but she gazed up at him with eyes bright with fever. "Sam?" she said. "Sam?"

"No, it's me, Tavin." He'd felt a twinge of desperate hope from her amid her confusion. He didn't know who Sam was, and at the moment, he did not care, for now he must see the extent of her wound and clean it, and attempt to keep her alive.

He slumped in exhaustion to the floor beside the basin of bloody water, his back against the bed frame. At some point, he'd managed to build a fire on the small hearth, and its warmth felt good all the way to his bones.

He was shaking from both exhaustion and the ordeal of tending to the lieutenant. In her lucid moments, she'd remained calm enough for him to sew up the parts of her wound needing it. *Physically* calm. Waves of pain, *her* pain washed over him, almost incapacitating him, but he'd gritted his teeth and worked through it. He hadn't felt the pain of her body exactly, but the impact of it on her.

She rested quietly for the moment, and he wanted nothing more than to stay by the fire and rest, too, but the horses were overdue for tending. He picked himself up and carried the basin out to dump it and collect fresh water to wash up in. When he stepped outside, it surprised him to find the sun rising, gray mist wafting along the forest floor. Then he stopped in his tracks and barely suppressed a cry, for he saw the figures of a few of the brigands on foot looking at the ground, their horses tethered a short distance away. They were just on the other side of where he believed the wards were located.

"The hoofprints just end," one of the men said in a weary voice. "Like they disappeared."

"It's some sort of trick," another said.

"Let's head back," the third said. "Not even worth it anymore. Besides, this is the queen's forest, and I've heard stories about the forester, that he's a giant and merciless." The man visibly shuddered.

The forester was a giant?

The man's companions did not seem up to arguing. They looked around some more, never crossing into the warded area, but returned to their horses in a desultory manner, mounted, and rode away. Tavin exhaled a breath he hadn't realized he'd been holding. He'd known the wards would not have allowed the men to cross, but he'd not been convinced of it until they left. Could they not even smell the smoke of his fire? He shook his head and continued with his chores.

He made sure the horses were comfortably settled in the covered paddock, all brushed down, fed, and watered. Bluebird had calmed down a good deal, but Tavin would keep checking on him. Last thing they needed was a horse colicking out of worry for his Rider.

Back inside, he found the lieutenant sleeping peacefully. He felt nothing else from her. He slid into a chair at the small table and rested his head on his arms. It hadn't been just the stitching of her rent flesh that had gotten to him. It was that he hadn't been around females much. Not that he hadn't wanted to be, but the times he tried . . . There was the one that he'd kissed, and her disgust at his touch had been like a slap. It had left him depressed for months, and he never wanted to know again what a girl thought of him.

He'd never really thought of the lieutenant, the Ice Lady, as female. He *knew* she was a woman, but he'd never thought of her like that. She was an officer surrounded by a wall of authority, one whom he'd rarely seen prior to this errand. He regarded her the same way as he might a statue of cold marble. It hit home, however, as he'd cut away her clothes, that she was definitely a *woman*. To be sure, her nakedness had not been the primary thing on his mind as he worked, but it was there nevertheless, and it was not a view he'd ever wanted of his lieutenant. It was unnerving to see the imposing officer, Queen Isen's favored Rider, so vulnerable. He'd felt embarrassed seeing her that way, and curious because he'd not really seen females unclothed.

That was not all he'd seen. There'd been scars, like stab wounds and cuts to her body. Being a queen's messenger was dangerous work, he'd been told time and again during training. You could take a fall from your horse, be sent into battle, or meet brigands along the road. Unfortunately, all he'd heard had become much too real.

Overcome by exhaustion, he dozed off. At first his sleep

was easy and dreamless, but then terrifying and full of fighting and blood and darkness. One image was so real, so present, and so disturbing he awoke with a cry. A mule, burdened with mail sacks, staggered toward him. It was not one of the mules that had been with the post rider they'd helped, for this one was an unusual white. Stains grew on the canvas of the mail sacks. Crimson stains. In the dream, he had not wanted to look, but he couldn't stop himself. He approached the mule and unbuckled one of the straps to open a sack. He started to look in, but before he could discern the contents, he awakened abruptly, his heart racing. It wasn't entirely the dream that had roused him, but a terrible, dawning grief. Tears flooded his eyes.

"No, no . . ." he murmured, and at that moment, he realized he was echoing the lieutenant, who was writhing beneath her blanket.

He moved to her side and saw tears on her cheeks glinting in the firelight.

"Sam," she murmured. "Sam." She settled for a moment, and did not awaken.

Tavin shook himself at the horror and grief stuck in the cobwebs of his mind.

Nightmare, he told himself, *that's all it is.* But had it been his, or hers? And the emotions had felt too real to be just a dream. He wished he had something to give her to allow her to sleep more deeply.

Her eyes opened and were fever bright. She stared right at him. "I will kill Urz and Torq. I *will.*"

The leaders of the Darrow Raiders, whom she had in fact

killed, or, at least, Urz. Rage surged with such ferocity through Tavin that he ran outside the cabin. A great yell of anguish erupted from deep within his chest. He leaned against a tree trunk, breathing hard and sobbing, and yelled again. It echoed through the forest.

There was a warming on his chest, which subsided quickly. He touched the spot and realized it was his winged horse brooch, the badge of the Green Riders. It hadn't done that since he first chose it—or *it chose him*—and pinned it on.

He'd always been sensitive to the people around him, picking up on moods and emotions. His uncle in a bad mood had always hit him like a storm wave. For the longest time he hadn't even known that other people weren't like him, that they couldn't pick up on the feelings of others like he could.

It had never been as intense as it had been just now, however, so pervasive, a gale that blew right through him. Perhaps the lieutenant's injury amplified her emotions. Whatever the case, he didn't think he'd be able to take much more. Fortunately, the gale slackened, and when he went back inside, he found the lieutenant to be resting peacefully.

He used the quiet time to turn extra bed sheets and shirts in the storage closet into bandages and make soup with some dried ingredients he found among the cabin's supplies, and herbs he found outside. When the lieutenant stirred, he decided it was time to change the dressings.

As he worked, she gazed at him with bleary hazel eyes. "We made it?" she whispered.

"We did," he replied. "North Waystation."

She closed her eyes again, seemed to drift off. Blood had

oozed through the old dressings, and he carefully pulled them away, dampening them where they crusted to her skin. She did not cry out in pain, but he nevertheless felt it, like a thousand pins jabbing him.

The wound was not pretty. His irregular stitches of blue thread against angry puckered flesh looked grotesque. It emanated heat. This was not good.

"I'm going to put some salve on this," he murmured more to himself than to her.

After he finished and rebandaged her wound, he tried to get her to take some broth from his soup, and water. She sipped a little water but refused the broth. He dabbed it onto her lips with a cloth, hoping to encourage her. He'd never imagined having to play nursemaid to the Ice Lady. But she wasn't really an Ice Lady, was she? Not in this condition, and if the despair and grief he had sensed from her earlier were any indication, then she had good reason to close herself against others.

When he finished, he kept himself busy, tending to the horses, sweeping the front step, repairing a couple shingles on the roof, and bringing in wood from the wood box. The lieutenant slept throughout the day, sometimes peacefully, sometimes fitfully.

When he was too tired to do more, he slipped a book out of his saddlebag. It was carefully wrapped in oilskin against the elements. It had been a gift to him from Granny Olsted, an elder and eccentric member of his village who had taken a shine to him. She was one of the few people who had shown him true kindness. She'd give him sweets or a kind word when she came to the inn, and he made sure to help her when he could, shoveling a path through the snow to her front door in winter, or fixing a shutter. He owned only a few books, and this was his favorite. It was called, *Ona-Holean-Lo: My Travels Through the Cloud Islands,* by Iver Harebody. The author had such a way with words that Tavin could almost taste the juicy *ongo* fruit, or see the topaz bays, the waves lapping against white sand beaches. The book carried him away to places he'd never been, such a relief when he most needed escape from his own world.

Granny Olsted had inscribed the frontispiece: *For my dear boy, Tavin, a book for an adventurous mind. I suspect you will go far.* He chuckled. He'd gone as far as Sacor City, and now North. If only the old dear could see him now.

Before he opened his book, a shelf with a few dusty volumes caught his eye. There were a couple novels. One was mouse chewed through several pages. A third was a logbook that appeared to contain entries made by other Green Riders who had stayed at the station over the years. He took this down to read and was amused by descriptions of outhouse mishaps—a snake on the seat, a beehive under the seat, an attempt to rescue a pair of specs dropped into the pit. There were also tales of various Riders' errands, notations about the weather, and stories of wildlife inhabiting the cabin.

The handwriting of the Riders was sometimes an almost illegible, crabbed script, and sometimes bold, but it swept him away to other times, other situations, much the same way *Ona-Holean-Lo* did. So much so, in fact, he was surprised to find it dark when he looked out the window.

He set the book aside to check on the lieutenant. She had been sleeping quietly, but now she moved restively on the bed. He placed his hand on her damp forehead and frowned.

"You're burning up," he murmured.

He tried to wake her, but she just moaned and pulled away. He needed to cool her down. He didn't want to be known as the green Greenie who killed his lieutenant on his first errand.

THE QUEEN'S FORESTER

As the evening wore on, the lieutenant's fever did not abate despite Tavin's efforts, and the waves of pain and confusion saturated with grief and anger that flowed from her buffeted him so that by late that night he was exhausted. He sat at the small table and lay his head down on his arms. He needed help. Where was the damn forester? Should he ride out to look for help? He could not leave her for the length of time it would take to reach North and return. He wished he were not alone.

Unable to rest, he sat back and saw still sitting on the table the logbook he'd been reading earlier. He opened it up to the last entry, turned to the next page, which was blank, then drew out his pen and ink. His pen scratched rapidly across the page as he described the attack by the brigands and the lieutenant's terrible wound.

After the fight, she ordered me to bring her to the waystation. We were chased by the brigands all the way from North. Lt. Mapstone's wound is festering

badly. She's burning with fever—don't know if
she'll live the night.

T. Bankside

Writing it down wasn't quite the same as telling someone
his troubles, but it helped him to feel a little less desolate. He
was about to add how alone and overwhelmed he felt, how
he was doing his best but desperately wished someone who
knew how to help her was there, but then she moaned. He
closed the logbook and went to her side. He could feel the
heat radiating off her. He reached for the cloth that he used
to dampen and cool her skin, but realized his bucket of water was empty.

"I'll be right back," he told her, even though he was pretty
sure she could not hear him.

"Sam," she murmured, blindly reaching for him.

"It's Tavin," he replied.

He placed her hand back across her belly and patted it.
"I'm going to fetch some water."

Her eyes cracked open with a glassy, hazel glint. Then
closed again and waves of yearning hit him. He grabbed the
bucket and rushed out of the cabin. Distance helped alleviate
the intensity some, but he'd have to go farther to completely
free himself of what he felt from her.

He stumbled through the dark to the spring and splashed
water on his face. Her yearning, the desire she projected, faded.
He shivered as the icy droplets fingered beneath his collar.

Back in the cabin, he attempted to cool her down. Otherwise there wasn't much he could do but refresh the water basin, bathe her fevered skin, and keep watch. He hadn't lied when he wrote in the logbook. He didn't know if she'd survive the night. It was looking less and less likely.

Eventually he dozed off on the floor beside the bed. Sheer exhaustion allowed him to sleep untroubled until the white mule staggered into his dreams again, blood stains spreading on the canvas mail sacks. Just as before, he approached the mule and unbuckled a sack, pushed the flap out of the way. He did not want to look, but the dream carried him on a current from which he could not turn. The grief began to well up in his chest again even before he could make sense of what he saw: a pair of hands, a man's hands, cut off at the wrist.

Sam? The plaintive query was not his own, and in the dream he tore open the other sacks and found additional severed body parts, including the man's head whose face he recognized from more amorous visions.

Sam, wailed over and over in explosive grief.

He woke screaming, and staggered outside in an attempt to distance himself from the pain flooding his mind, but he stumbled off the front step and was swallowed into a black well of grief.

"Green Rider?"

The bass voice was gentle and came to Tavin out of the dark. Gentle, but could call down thunder at will, he thought.

"Green Rider, you are not well," the voice said.

Tavin's eyes fluttered open. He could not make out much in the dark, but he sensed a very large presence that knelt beside him. Strong hands helped him rise to a sitting position and gave him a sip of water. He drank eagerly.

"Easy," the man said. "Take it slow."

Images of horror still flashed through Tavin's mind, but the deep well of grief was gone. He felt only tranquility. The lieutenant must be sleeping, and the man who helped him? Calm rolled off him like the ocean on a quiet day.

"You the forester?" Tavin asked. His throat was sore as though he'd been screaming.

"Yes, Rider. I am Abram Rust, queen's forester."

"I'm Tavin. Tavin Bankside."

"I meant to come sooner," the forester said, "but I had to chase some brigands out of the woods. There has been much lawlessness since the fall of the Darrow Raiders. Others, gangs of them, trying to claim their place and power."

"The lieutenant—" Tavin said, forcing himself to his feet. Abram also stood and steadied him. At full height, the forester seemed a giant.

"I have been in to see her," Abram replied, "and saw her grave wounds. I have tended her best as I can for the forest provides many gifts, including medicinal herbs, but my skills are limited. She needs the help of a mender."

"Where am I to find a mender?" Tavin asked. "She ordered me not to return to North, and she might not make it long enough for me to go anyway."

"No, not North. There are none there with enough skill

to heal her. There may be one who is closer. Come, let us go in."

Once inside, Abram seemed to fill the cabin. His head brushed the rafters. Tavin could better make out his crinkled features in the candlelight. Curly whiskers reminiscent of the stringy lichens that hung off trees covered much of his face. Piercing black eyes beneath bushy brows regarded him in return. Beneath his cloak, embroidered into a weathered leather jerkin was an evergreen. Definitely the queen's forester. A huge ax, among other implements, hung from his broad belt.

He turned to the lieutenant, who slept mostly peacefully, her cheeks too red, and only a sheet over her to keep her cooler and retain some modesty. A wholesome herby scent wafted in the air, and the basin beside her bed glimmered with fresh water.

"I thank you for tending her while I was . . ."

"Insensible?" Abram provided. "I see no injury upon you. Is there something I am missing?"

"Um, no."

"Hmm." Abram removed a pipe from his belt pouch. "Might you tell me what happened? And then you can take a rest before you go looking for the hermit in the morning."

"What hermit?"

"The one who can heal Laren." Abram sat in one of the chairs by the fire. It creaked alarmingly.

Tavin sat in the other, and told Abram of their encounter with the brigands and the nightmarish flight to reach the

waystation. Blue tendrils of pipe smoke wove around Abram's head as Tavin spoke.

When he finished, Abram said, "You fought bravely and have done well by your lieutenant. You did not mention the use of your special ability. Now, no need for denials, Rider, I am quite familiar with Green Riders and the fact they are gifted with small magics augmented by the brooches they wear. Winged horses." A smoke ring floated into the rafters.

"I don't really know what my ability is," Tavin said. "Hasn't shown up yet."

Another smoke ring was set adrift. "Are you so sure?"

"Yes." He hadn't suddenly developed the ability to walk through a wall or create fire. A true healing ability, he thought, would be useful about now.

Abram did not comment but sucked on his pipe and gazed into space. Eventually he said, "When I first met Laren, she did not know her ability either. It was near the end of her first year, if I recall correctly. Quite a determined young lady. Why, once when she was accosted in North, she left three big lumberjacks flattened in the dirt and it was the talk of the town for ages." He chuckled and his whole body shook. When he settled, he added, "I always saw an important future for her. We must make sure she survives."

"What kind of future?" Tavin asked, interested despite himself.

"Mind, I have no gift of foresight," Abram admitted, "but she is a leader. She has that quality about her. And she's a good friend to young Prince Zachary, and has the ear of the queen. She led the fight to destroy the Darrow Raiders. I can't help but think she is important to Sacoridia's future."

"Huh." As far as Tavin knew, most Green Riders were released by their brooches within four or five years. If they didn't die first. She'd exceeded that. He glanced at her once more. Helpless and vulnerable as she was, it was hard to see her as a leader. Hard to believe she'd been behind the defeat of the Darrow Raiders. He couldn't see the future either, however, and he shrugged.

"Well, now, you are exhausted," Abram said. "You must rest now, and I'll watch over the both of you."

"What if she doesn't make it through the night?"

"Laren Mapstone has some fight left in her," Abram said quietly. "But it is not endless, which is why you must go to the hermit first thing in the morning."

A SICK MIND

When Tavin awoke the next morning where he'd bedded down next to the paddock, he was startled to discover Abram towering over him.

"She made it through the night," the forester said, "but she's not doing so well now."

Tavin scrubbed his face. He knew. He'd taken his bedroll out by the horses hoping to get a little distance from the lieutenant's emotions and dreams, all laden with such grief and violence that even the calm Abram exuded did not block it. Being by the horses helped enough to allow him some fitful sleep. But now Bluebird pawed the ground and circled. Goose nuzzled him as though to help calm him.

Tavin shed his blankets and followed Abram to the front of the cabin and sat on the step. Abram handed him a bowl of hot oats supplemented with blueberries and nuts from the woods.

"Thanks," Tavin mumbled.

"You must set out to find the hermit as soon as you finish," Abram said. "I will stay with Laren and tend her with what herb knowledge I possess."

The oats were really good. Abram had drizzled honey over them. "How do I find this hermit?"

Abram squinted up at the fair patches of sky through interwoven tree branches. "Well, that's the trick, isn't it." His piercing gaze then landed firmly on Tavin. "You must seek the spirit of the wood, and when you find it, you will find the hermit."

Tavin paused with a spoonful of oats before his mouth. "What in the hells does that mean?"

"The Green Cloak is very old," Abram replied, "and in some ways deeper and more powerful than is known, even in these days when there is little magic left in the world. Pockets of that ancient power remain throughout."

"Is the hermit some kind of mage?"

Abram stroked fingers thoughtfully through his beard. "He has been here longer than I, much longer, and that is saying something. Still, I do not know precisely who or what he is. He will tell you he is a wanderer."

Tavin scraped the last of the oats out of the bowl and set it beside him on the step. This was ridiculous. All the magic had left the world during the Scourge following the Long War a thousand years ago. Everyone knew that. And yet, he mused, the Green Riders had persisted, individuals with such minor magic that their abilities surfaced only when they heard the call and were chosen by a gold winged horse brooch. He frowned. If Green Riders had endured through the centuries, it wasn't a great leap to suppose that others with magic had, as well.

When a sudden surge of disorientation set the world to

spinning around him, he knew the lieutenant's fever had spiked. "How do I find the spirit of the wood?"

Abram, who also seemed to pick up on the lieutenant's distress at the same moment, replied, "It is not so much a thing you look for as a sense. Go into the woods. Open your mind to the forest. Let your thoughts be as the wind drifting among the branches and beneath the canopy. Put aside your cares and feel peace, and set your intention to seek the hermit. Breathe deep. Only then will the path become clear to you."

Tavin was incredulous. "My thoughts be as the wind?" What the hells did *that* mean?

Abram did not answer for he had already entered the cabin. Tavin rose to follow, but another wave of disorientation threw him off balance and he stumbled off the step. Gritting his teeth, and trying to force the disorientation away, he staggered inside. Abram patted the lieutenant's face with a wet cloth. She murmured and moved restively beneath her sheet.

Abram looked up at him. His expression was one of concern. His whiskers drooped. "I will keep watch and care for her as I can, but we are running out of time. You must go now."

"But I don't understand. Which way?"

"Direction does not matter. Go into the wood and do as I instructed. And do not forget payment for the hermit. Offer him your most precious possession."

"I do not have much," Tavin said.

"It is not the how much that matters," Abram said. "It is the *what*."

Tavin grabbed his pack and shortcoat from a chair. "The most precious thing I have is Goose."

"The hermit will not be wanting your horse. Leave him here. You go now. If you wait too long, even the hermit will be unable to help her. Go to the woods and open your mind."

Tavin left the cabin. He walked away from it, could hear Bluebird worrying in the paddock. Goose nickered after him. He strode through the wards that concealed the waystation and into the woods stepping over fallen trees. Brush snagged his clothes. He wanted a nap, explicit directions as to where he must go. He needed it all to be spelled out for him. It was madness, a fanciful quest built on gossamer wings. Was Abram cracked? No, he seemed perfectly in command of his faculties, and the lieutenant had spoken highly of him.

At least the lieutenant's emotional impact on him faded with every step he took. That was a relief in itself. He paused to look over his shoulder. The cabin had already vanished from sight. He wondered if he'd be able to find his way back after he found the hermit.

He walked until he came to a sunny clearing with bald granite bedrock as its floor, moss fringing its edges and the seams, and round patches of blue-green lichen crusting its surface. He dropped his pack and sat in the middle with his legs sprawled before him. He reveled in the sunshine and the quiet in his mind. Birds piped and trilled from branches, and small creatures rustled in the leaf-litter and underbrush nearby. Such a relief to be away from the lieutenant. She would, he reflected, be embarrassed to learn he had experienced all her grief and nightmares. She had contained it all for so long, had worked so long to control her outward appearance. This was why, he realized, others perceived her as the Ice Lady. She believed she could not allow herself to let down her façade of control or share her deeper self with others because of her position. In her mind, doing so would make her appear weak. It was her excuse, really, so she wouldn't have to face the pain inside her.

He shook his head. It took a life-threatening wound and fever for her to face her pain, and he had the misfortune of being the one with her when she did.

So now he must sit in this clearing and somehow sense the spirit of the wood. He lay back on the sun-warmed rock and gazed at the sky, the puffy clouds drifting across the opening of the clearing, his view framed by the crowns of towering spruce and fir.

He must find the spirit of the wood, and in so doing, he would find the hermit. It was absurd, but what if what Abram said was true? He'd be condemning the lieutenant to death if he didn't try, and there was no harm in trying.

He lay there listening to the music of the forest, the song of birds, the creak of trees swaying in the breeze. Insects buzzing by. His eyes sagged closed at the peacefulness of it all. Only an irritation scratching at the edge of his mind kept him from falling asleep, and it was a good thing because it warned him someone else was nearby, and it was not likely to be the hermit, for the feeling that came with the irritation was one of cruelty and hate, and carried with it a familiar tang. It was one of the men who had pursued him and the lieutenant from North.

He rose to his feet and carried his pack out of the clearing into the trees so he'd be better concealed. He drew his longknife and waited.

He could not tell from which direction the enemy was coming, only that he was nearing. Tavin sensed the man's persistence, that he would not allow a pair of the bitch queen's Greenies to best him. He would bring their heads back to show off to his gang. He'd have vengeance for their interference with the robbery of the post rider. Not just vengeance, but an enjoyment of torture and killing. A sick mind, Tavin thought. Even if the waystation was warded and concealed from others besides Green Riders and one particular forester, he was very glad Abram was with the lieutenant lest the brigand search in that direction.

The hateful emotions only intensified. Tavin clung close to the trunk of a pine and peered through the woods. There was not a lot of undergrowth for the canopy was thick, but the trunks of trees were many and he could see no one.

He started to turn to look the other way when he heard the crack of a branch. He froze, then turned the rest of the way. The man was across the clearing and they saw each other at the same time.

The man charged, knife drawn. He radiated eagerness. His nostrils flared. Tavin braced himself and grunted at not only the physical impact but also that of a man's glee to kill. A glee the man knew well. He liked to kill. They slammed to the ground and struggled.

Images flowed from the man into Tavin's mind—memories of his first kill when he was a boy. He'd lured an even younger boy into an abandoned barn and stabbed him. He'd been fascinated by what lay beneath the skin.

Tavin rolled to evade a thrust of the knife, tried to push and kick the man off him. He'd lost hold of his own knife. He could feel the man's emotions, but not discern his next move.

More memory-images poured into him. As the boy grew into a youth, he became bored of luring his victims to him. Instead, he turned to hunting, stalking his prey for days, if not months. Patience, patience, then trapping a young woman as she hurried along a quiet street at night. Lovely and well-loved. He'd learned all about her, his prey, to better track her. The more well-loved the prey, the greater the impact on those who knew her, the more dynamic the thrill of the kill, the art of it.

Tavin grappled and punched ineffectively at the man. They rolled over roots and rocks and pine needles. He gripped the man's wrist to stop the knife from plunging into his chest.

When stalking easy prey became boring, the man rode with the Darrow Raiders, who were amused by his blood thirst and desire to hunt more difficult prey. They liked his inventiveness when it came to the torture and slaughter of Green Riders, and others, including a certain post rider. They had known that the Red Witch, which was what they called Lieutenant Mapstone, and this post rider were a couple. Not just a couple, but lovers. It was the man's idea to cut up the post rider and send him to his postmaster in the mailbags. They had laughed about it and knew that it would be a strike against the Red Witch who had read their minds and hunted them for the queen. They made the post rider's death as extended and torturous as possible.

Tavin cried out even before the knife bit into his shoulder. He pushed the man off him and scrambled to his feet, breathing hard. The man crouched, ready to leap, his knife poised.

"You killed Sam," Tavin said. "It was you."

"Who? I've killed lots of people."

"I know. He was a post rider."

"Killed more than a few of those," the man said, relishing his memories. "But I bet you mean the Red Witch's man, eh? Heh, we butchered him good. All my idea to send him back in his mailbags. I hear she was there when the mule got to his postmaster. Wish I'd been there to see her face."

It had all been too much, being the receptacle for all the lieutenant's unfiltered pain, the grief she had contained so long. Now for that of this man who visited such terror upon his victims and was amused by their suffering, and who experienced something akin to sexual arousal when he killed.

"Where's your horse, Greenie?" the man asked. "I'll cut you up like I did the Witch's man and send you back to the bitch queen."

His excitement at the prospect barreled into Tavin's mind. Tavin clenched his fists. "No more," he whispered.

"What you say? You praying to the gods or asking for mercy?"

The man would love to hear him beg for mercy. "No more," he replied more loudly.

"We're just beginning." The man laughed, and then rushed Tavin.

Tavin was not sure what he did, or how he did it, but he pulled out all the emotions and pain of the man's victims he'd witnessed in the memories, and combined them with the grief of the lieutenant and poured them into the man in such a way that he would experience it all from the victims' point of view. At first the man froze in surprise, then he dropped to the ground howling.

THE LANGUAGE
OF SQUIRRELS

As the man writhed on the ground and moaned, the world blurred and dimmed around Tavin. The next thing he knew, he was face down in a clump of moss and felt as if he were awakening from a long sleep. But no, he'd been weakened and then . . . fell unconscious? Weakened by what? By disgorging all that emotion back into his attacker? Had he really done that? He rose onto his hands and knees and found the man still rolling on the ground and clawing at his eyes. His tears ran red with blood.

Tavin unsteadily climbed to his feet and sagged against a tree trunk. He was exhausted and . . . empty. All that the man had imposed on him was gone, including his current agony. The effect of the lieutenant's emotions on Tavin had also been alleviated. For once in his life, no one's emotions other than his own intruded on his mind.

"Make it stop, please, make it stop," the man said between sobs. "I'm sorry, I'm sorry. Please, make it stop."

Tavin looked down on him and squashed any stirrings of pity. The man was a monster, and it served him right to suffer.

"Please . . ."

"No," Tavin said, and he picked up his pack, found his longknife and sheathed it. He threw the brigand's knife as far into the woods as he could. Then, he walked away. The farther away he got, the lighter he felt. He certainly retained some increment of the emotions he'd received from the lieutenant and the murderer, but they were more a memory of them than the actual experience.

How was he to find the hermit now, though? And, were there other brigands he might encounter? He may have found some measure of peace from the emotions of others, but he'd his own to contend with, the excitement of the fight, the uncertainty over what he'd done to the murderer. And only then did he begin to feel the pain in his shoulder. When he touched it, his fingers came away bloody. When he probed it some more, it did not seem to be deep. He halted, removed his shortcoat, and poured water over the wound from his waterskin and hissed at the sting. He bound a handkerchief around it best as he could.

What now? How much time had all this wasted? In how much more danger was the lieutenant? Could Abram keep her alive? Alive long enough to find some mysterious old hermit by feeling the spirit of the wood?

A red squirrel bounded on a tree limb overhead and scolded him.

"Nuisance," he muttered.

The squirrel dropped an object that hit Tavin between his eyes.

"Ow!"

He gazed at the ground. It was littered with the acorns of previous seasons. The squirrel chittered.

"Brat."

The squirrel chirped at him and bounded from one branch to another as if to encourage him to follow.

Tavin shook his head and moved on. As he walked, he wondered if leaving the murderer behind was the right thing to do. It had felt right at the time, but now he was less sure. Leaving the man to continue reliving all the horror he'd caused from the point of view of his victims probably wasn't the merciful thing to do, though one could argue he had never shown any of *his* victims mercy. Still, Tavin could not help but wonder if his act made him no better than that man.

No, I do not hunt, torture, and kill innocent people, he thought. *I was defending myself.*

Except for the last part where the man begged him for mercy.

He then wondered what would happen if the emotional torment released the man. Might he become changed, a more altruistic person? Or would he just be angrier and try to hunt Tavin down in vengeance? Tavin guessed the latter, but the truth was he had no idea what he'd unleashed and how long it would last, or what the final outcome might be, but once again he'd felt a rightness to what he'd done. At last, the man's victims had received some form of justice.

He was surprised the squirrel continued to move along with him from tree to tree. It squabbled at him if he paused.

At least he was pretty sure it was the same squirrel. As he continued, the character of the forest changed. Leafy birches, maples, beeches, and oaks supplanted evergreens, and he waded through patches of ferns. More squirrels joined the first one skittering among the branches and chirped as if to encourage him to keep going. When he stopped to rest by a stream and wash his face, he was pelted with multiple acorns.

"What the hells?" he demanded.

They chastised him until he stood and moved on. He walked alongside the stream with his peculiar escort. When he thought to cross the stream, they harangued him so incessantly that he did not. When he experimented with walking away from the stream, they showered him with acorns and spruce cones.

"All right, all right," he muttered, and continued walking alongside the stream.

The squirrels were clearly directing him, but to what end it was impossible say. He hoped they were taking him to the hermit. Why else would a pack of crazy squirrels herd him along in this manner? It wasn't any stranger than anything else that had happened this day. He had never imagined, however, that this was the form the spirit of the wood would take on. So much for letting his mind "be as the wind drifting among the branches and beneath the canopy," as Abram had put it. Being pelted by acorns when you deviated from the desired path cast it in an entirely different light. In any event, he had not found the spirit of the wood; *it* had found him.

Soon he came to a bright glade. A breeze riffled emerald grasses and ferns, and the trill of the winter wren rang out to greet him. In the center of the glade stood a humongous oak. Its trunk was as wide as Goose was long, if not more so, its branches and bark gnarled and craggy like a very, very old man presiding over the youngsters of the forest.

The squirrels chittered and scattered, all but a few leaving him alone in the glade.

I guess I am here, he thought, *but if this is the hermit's place, where is he?*

He felt no other human presence, nor saw evidence of such.

"Hello?"

He walked around the great oak stepping carefully over its immense roots. On the back side was a crevice in its trunk. The interior was alight with sunshine and thus hollow, and yet, the immense limbs, which were big enough to be huge trees in their own right, lived festooned in leafy splendor bearing bunches of young, green acorns. Birds flitted from branch to branch, and a blue jay bellowed its territorial call. Squirrels ran along on their own business. From a cavity above Tavin's head, an owl peered out.

When he circled back to his starting place, he found a man standing in the glade. Tall and lanky, his skin the smooth brown of an acorn, he wore a headdress of deer antlers with leaves and twigs woven around its crown. A chickadee perched on one of the antlers, and a spider web shimmered between the tines of the other. He fed birds seed from his hands, and was simply attired in short pants and a billowy shirt. His expression was rapturous as he tweeted and whistled at the birds. What Tavin had first taken to be a fur collar the man wore turned out to be a big gray squirrel snuggled around his neck.

Tavin had to shake himself to make sure he wasn't bespelled and seeing things. "Hello," he said tentatively. "Are you the hermit?"

The man looked up at him, and Tavin was taken by eyes that were more gold than brown, the ancient depth of them that nevertheless held bright merriment. When he realized his mouth was hanging open, he shut it.

"Am I *the* hermit?" the man asked, considering. "Well, well, let us see. I live away from people and rarely see them. By that description, I suppose I am the hermit, or at least *a* hermit. There are others, you know. But I don't really live alone, do I? I have all my friends here, and they are enough."

The urgency of Tavin's mission came back to him, and the words tumbled out of his mouth. "My name is Tavin Bankside. I am a Green Rider, and Abram, the queen's forester, sent me to find you. You see, my lieutenant was badly wounded and she needs a mender."

"You could have gone to North," the hermit said. "There are one or two there, or so I hear."

"Abram sent me to you."

"Abram is a good soul. One of the few I welcome to the glade. But I am very busy, young Tavin."

Tavin glanced about and saw nothing that indicated busyness. "Please, she's very ill, my lieutenant, and may soon die."

A squirrel chattered from a branch overhead. The hermit glanced up and responded with a very convincing squirrel-

K. Britain

like reply. Some sort of animated discussion ensued complete with displays of foot thumping, body twitches, and hopping by both parties. Tavin had never seen the like.

"Uh, excuse me," he broke in, "but did you hear me? She could die."

The hermit paused his conversation. "Did you know the language of squirrels is very complex? You get one accent wrong and you are telling the squirrel to stuff their acorns someplace other than their cheeks." His gaze then turned more serious. "I knew of your presence in the wood as soon as you entered it, young Tavin. Your aura cast far and wide to any who are sensitive to such resonances. I also know what you did to the brigand who wished to murder you. A very bad man, one of several whose mere existence have been leaving a stain in the forest. Sunshine here," and he indicated the squirrel aloft, "has explained the situation of your unfortunate lieutenant. I am fluent in Squirrel, you see."

Tavin's patience and wonderment were quickly fading. "Can you help her, please?"

"Probably I could. Have you brought payment?"

"I—I don't have a lot," Tavin replied. He emptied his purse. Four coppers and a silver.

The hermit stroked the squirrel on his shoulder. "Coins, eh? Is that all your lieutenant is worth to you?"

"What? Well, no, but you wanted payment."

"Payment does not always mean coins, young Tavin. What else have you?"

"Um . . ." Tavin unshouldered his pack and emptied the contents on the ground. There were his travel rations and a mess kit, a hat for the rain, a comb, a sweater for cool nights, an assortment of handkerchiefs, and the book Granny Olsted had given him, among other small items.

The hermit picked through his belongings. "A hoof pick won't do me much good." He tossed it aside and examined the comb. He tried to comb his mustache. "Hum." Then he cast it away. He looked close at the hardtack and dried meat and made a face. He seemed to like the sweater, but then put it aside, as well.

Tavin's heart fell when the hermit picked up the book and flipped through the pages and seemed interested. The hermit gave him a sidelong and canny look.

"This has great value to you."

"Yes, it does," Tavin replied. "It was given to me by the only person who ever really cared about me when I was growing up."

The hermit opened the book and read the inscription. "A story of travels in the Cloud Islands, eh? I last saw them as volcanoes just steaming out of the ocean."

"What?" Tavin said.

"You are willing to give me this book, this prized possession, to help your lieutenant?"

Tavin nodded, his heart falling. It was just a book, he told himself. He could replace it. But a replacement wouldn't have Granny Olsted's words in it. A replacement would not be a well-meant gift, and really, the only one he had ever received. And would it be a kind of betrayal to give it away?

"I will hold onto it," the hermit said, "and I will take the silver coin."

"I thought you said payment doesn't always mean coins."

"I didn't say I wouldn't take one."

Tavin tried to hide his annoyance and passed the strange man the silver.

The hermit flipped it on his hand. "It's not for me. It's for the crows. They like the shineys." He held his hand open, and a crow swooped down and landed on his wrist. It took the coin in its beak and launched into the air with the flutter of blue-black wings.

Damnation, Tavin thought. What a waste. He could have used that silver, and the hermit had just thrown it away.

"They bring me such interesting gifts," the hermit said, gazing after the crow. "Little bones, pretty pebbles smoothed by the stream, even pieces of broken glass and a button or two. It is nice to give them something in return."

Tavin, still stung by the loss of his book, and now his silver coin, stuffed his scattered belongings into his pack.

"Your pack will be lighter now," the hermit said.

Tavin grunted. The observation did not make him feel any better.

"I must collect my own bag," the hermit told him.

Tavin followed him to the crack in the oak tree. The hermit slipped through it. It was so narrow Tavin would not have fit, so he didn't even try to follow. In fact, as he thought about it, it seemed too narrow even for the skinny hermit, but somehow he'd gotten through. When the hermit reemerged, Tavin's eyes couldn't quite make sense of how he managed it. The hermit had left behind his headdress and slung a simple cloth bag over his shoulder. It was woven in an astonishing array of colorful threads in no discernible pattern.

"Do you live in there?" Tavin asked, nodding toward the crack.

The hermit chuckled. "You mean like an Eletian Sleeper?"

"What? Eletians are just legends."

"So short are mortal lives," the hermit mused as though to himself, "that if they cannot see a thing, it is not there." Then directly to Tavin he said, "The oak allows me entrance for we are old friends, but no, I do not live within. All manner of other creatures do call it home, however. But me, I live in a small cabin. A hermit's cabin if you will."

"Well, uh, better to live in a cabin," Tavin said. "I mean, the tree looks like it's rotted inside. A cabin is safer."

"Rotted? Nah. A structure made by a man safer?" The hermit shook his head. "Hardly. This oak is ancient, young Tavin. It has stood for three or four thousand years and remains strong and true. I trust in nature far more than in man."

The hermit prickled Tavin the wrong way, but the lieutenant needed his mending skills. "Can we go, please?"

The hermit lifted the somnolent squirrel from his shoulder and set it by the base of the oak. The squirrel stretched, then ran up the trunk.

"Old Raincloud has become rather lazy," the hermit said, "eating his fill of acorns and sleeping all day."

With that, they at last set off across the glade.

"I am not sure I know the way back to the waystation," Tavin said.

"It is of no trouble to find. We go the way you came, and look for what is not there."

"What? Oh, you mean the wards."

"Yes, yes," the hermit replied, his strides long and swift. "The wards hide the waystation creating null space in the forest. And never fear, we will arrive in no time. Nothing in this forest is far from the great oak."

WOUNDS

As they followed the stream, the hermit paused to pick plants and drop them into his bag. He hummed to himself and sang each time he found a plant he liked.

"Tickleweed, tickleweed," he sang, "good for the tickle in the lungs, the wheezing and the cough." When he found a patch of watercress growing in a stream, he stuffed a bunch into his mouth. "Good for the eating, good for mixing with greens."

Dragonflies seemed to delight in hovering around him. Sunlight glistened on glassy wings as they flittered and bobbed on gentle currents of air. A few squirrels followed, scampering along on their own branching pathways.

"Tsk, tsk," the hermit said when they came upon a decaying old oak. "But nature's gifts are great even in the dying." On one side of the rotting trunk they found yellow-orange shelf fungus growing. "The folk in North call it Chicken of the Woods." He proceeded to harvest some of it with his knife. "We will have a very nice soup of it tonight."

The hermit's bag was bulging by the time they turned from the stream. They walked a short while before Tavin discerned, to his dismay, the clearing ahead where he had fought the murderer. The hermit was making a beeline for it.

"Can't we go around it?" Tavin asked.

"No, I must see for myself." The lightness was gone from the hermit's voice.

When they reached the edge of the clearing, he immediately located the murderer. It was odd, Tavin thought, he felt nothing from him. The man lay unmoving, curled into a fetal position, and the stench of released bowels hung in the air. Blood leaked from his nose, mouth, and ears. His eyes were missing, and flies swarmed around the raw sockets.

Tavin turned away and gagged. "Animals have gotten to him."

"No, not yet," the hermit said. "His eyes are in his hands."

Tavin threw up. Afterward, with a sick, sour taste in his mouth, he realized it was all his doing. He had killed the man by pushing all those emotions and memories on him.

"It would appear, young Tavin," the hermit said, "the emotional surge was too much for him and it stopped his heart." Then more lightly he added, "The animals will find him soon enough and what is left will nourish the earth."

"Can we keep moving?" Tavin asked, eager to leave the scene. "We can't waste any more time. My lieutenant needs help."

"Are you sure," the hermit asked with a knowing look, "that it is your lieutenant who needs help?"

"That man was a murderer. He killed lots of people and liked it. He was trying to kill me and so I—I—"

"Did what you had to and defended yourself in, shall we say, an unexpected way?"

Tavin nodded. The hermit seemed to know so much.

"The murderer," said the hermit, "received exactly the punishment he deserved."

Taken aback, Tavin searched the hermit's face for a hint of mockery or reproof, but found none. He wasn't sure what he saw, whether it was ancient wisdom, or the canniness of one who had seen much in the world, or maybe one who understood him better than Tavin understood himself.

A crow cackled in a birch nearby.

The hermit brightened. "It is time for our friends to feast as they will. Let us go now to your lieutenant."

Tavin looked up. The near trees were filled with crows waiting. Waiting and watching with their sharp obsidian eyes. He shuddered and followed the hermit away from the corpse and those who would feed.

He felt the lieutenant's pain and disorientation before they reached the wards that concealed the waystation. Her emanations indicated how weak and tired she was. She hadn't much fight left in her. The solid feeling he had gotten from Abram remained, which was reassuring.

"She's still alive," Tavin murmured.

"Yes," the hermit replied. When they stepped through the wards, the hermit giggled. "It tickles."

Not exactly the way Tavin would describe it, but to each his own.

The cabin appeared the same as it had when he had left that morning. Goose called out to him with an anxious neigh, and Bluebird still worried around the little paddock. A squirrel jumped from a tree limb to the paddock roof, descended down a post, and sat on the fence where it and Goose regarded one another.

When they entered the cabin, Tavin staggered backward at the miasma of illness, of festering flesh, that suffused the air. The lieutenant was ghastly pale in contrast to her red hair. Her lips moved, but she'd no strength to speak. Abram looked relieved by their arrival, but his features were still drawn.

"She has taken a turn for the worse," he said.

The hermit sidled by him and leaned over the bed. Curiously he sniffed the air above the lieutenant, then placed his hand, with its long, thin fingers, on her forehead. For a moment she seemed to stir.

"Can you help her?" Tavin asked.

"Perhaps, perhaps not," was the maddening response. "Had you fetched me any later, definitely not."

"Rider," Abram said, "I have not been able to tend the horses as I should. They've had their morning feed and fresh water, but that is all."

Tavin understood. He was not needed or wanted in the cabin while the hermit worked, and it was a relief. He nodded and stepped outside and took a deep breath of air that was free of sickness. When he entered the paddock, he patted

Goose, but went to Bluebird who circled and had sweat foaming on his neck.

"Easy, boy," he said. "That man I brought is a mender and he's going to help her. He's a little strange and talks to squirrels, but I think . . . I think he'll be able to help her."

As if to reinforce his words, the squirrel, now sitting on a fence post with a spruce cone, jabbered its opinion.

"I need you to settle," he told Bluebird. "You colicking isn't going to help her. You have to be strong for her. All right?"

Bluebird's ears flopped morosely and he shook his head. Tavin took out a brush and worked on the gelding's hide, talking to him the entire time. It seemed to calm both of them. When he was done, Bluebird accepted a handful of grain from him, swished his tail, and took a drink of water. He kept close by as Tavin turned to Goose, who quivered his hide in pleasure at the attention.

That accomplished, he shoveled their droppings out of the paddock, checked their water once more, then found a sunny place in front of the cabin to sit, and eventually lie down on a soft carpet of moss as he awaited word.

He swatted at a biter buzzing around his face. Then he shivered with a chill. The sun had moved leaving him in the shade. Nearby, the hermit sat, legs crossed, reading the book. Once more, Tavin felt a pang for its loss, but it was well worth the sacrifice if the hermit's mending skills helped the lieutenant.

"How is she?" he asked. He could feel nothing from her.

A butterfly perched atop the hermit's head working its wings. Without looking up from his reading, the hermit replied, "She is resting quietly."

"Will she—?"

"Live? We shall see. We shall see. I drained and cleaned the festering, and have treated the wounds with poultices and a paste that will draw out and fight the infection. Speaking of which, I will take care of your shoulder."

Tavin glanced at the forgotten wound with its makeshift bandage. "It's all right."

"No one knows where the blade that nicked you has been, eh? Except the bad man and he is dead."

As he applied an herby paste to the wound—the same he'd used on the lieutenant, he informed Tavin—and wrapped a bandage around Tavin's shoulder, he said, "Not so bad, unlike your lieutenant. That is some sewing job you did on her, my friend. If she survives, she will never forget you."

Great, Tavin thought. If she survived, he would apologize.

"You kept her alive, though." The hermit knotted the bandage. "That is what counts. You kept her alive until I could come."

"Abram did, too."

"Yes, and Abram, who has gone to look for more of the bad men."

"By himself?"

"He is scouting. He cannot take on all of them, and the folk of North will do nothing about them. He can at least know where they are and confront those who enter the queen's forest. They are a poison to the spirit of the wood, those bad men, like a suppurating wound. Overhunting, cutting down trees of great age without a thought, robbing and murdering." He smacked Tavin on his injured shoulder.

"OW!"

"You'll be fine. At least in regard to that scratch. Now about your lieutenant. If she starts to improve, there is only so much I can do for her physical healing. She will need you to help with the rest."

Tavin rubbed his still smarting shoulder. "What can I do? I am no mender."

"No, my friend, but you've a gift that will help her cope with the very dark suffering her wounds have released. You know of what I speak?"

"What the Darrow Raiders, that man I killed, did to the one she loved? And to her friends?"

The hermit nodded solemnly. "These hurts are as potent and painful as any wound to the flesh, and harder to treat."

"But what the hells kind of gift are you talking about?"

"I think you know. You are all but bleeding out an empathic gift."

"You mean feeling what other people feel?" Tavin shook his head. "Nothing special about that. I've done it forever since I was born, I think. It's normal, but I hate it."

The hermit raised his eyebrows. "Young Tavin, it is anything but normal. It is extraordinary, and that Green Rider trinket of yours has only made it stronger. The man in the clearing, for instance."

Tavin's hand went to his brooch. *"This* is my special ability? The same thing that has cursed me my entire life?"

"Cursed? No, it is a rare—"

"Feeling everyone's emotions? My uncle in a rage? The girls who were disgusted by me?" Tavin pointed back at the cabin. "All her grief? I have feelings of my own, but I don't get to deal with them because I have to deal with everyone else's. And now you are telling me that my Rider ability is the same thing, but stronger? Well, isn't this a load of stinking horse crap?"

He stood and stormed off into the woods. To the hermit's credit, he did not attempt to follow.

Tavin found a rocky ledge some distance from the cabin. He held his brooch in his hand. It gleamed in the late afternoon light. It was a betrayal. He'd wanted a useful special ability, the ability to see far, or maybe ignite fire with his hands, but no. It was just more of the same that had made him miserable his whole life. What use was it to him? Well, it had warned him to the presence of brigands, but that was all. It had only otherwise brought him pain. He thought about the day before when the lieutenant's emotions seemed to break his mind, and that's when he guessed his ability had emerged. Or, if not exactly emerged because he already had it, gained strength.

He clenched his hand around his brooch and hurled it as

far as he could. It clacked against a tree or rock somewhere in the distance. *To the hells with all this.*

He noted a squirrel watching him intently from a branch. So, the hermit hadn't followed him, but had sent one of his spies. He scooped up a rock and threw it at the squirrel, and missed of course. The squirrel scolded him soundly and stomped on its branch.

"Tell your master to mind his own business," Tavin yelled, and he threw another rock for good measure.

The squirrel expressed its wrath with such vocal convulsions that Tavin thought the little creature might rupture its spleen, and he suspected there were more than a few Squirrelish expletives being hurled his way. Eventually the squirrel silenced itself, bounded along its branch, and leaped to the next tree and away.

Tavin laughed bitterly at himself. He was not feeling anything from anyone else, but his own emotions were intense and unpleasant. He lingered for a while longer, until he cooled down, then trudged back toward the cabin without bothering to look for his brooch. If what the other Riders said was true, it would find him soon enough.

THE FRACTURED MIRROR

It was dusk by the time Tavin returned to the cabin. Candle-light glowed in the window. As he approached, a squirrel perched on the roof's overhang harangued him.

"Sorry I threw the rock at you," he said, assuming it was the same one. "It's not your fault I'm cursed."

The squirrel, not so easily appeased and with much more to say, bristled its tail and railed at him at length. Tavin shook his head and no sooner set his foot on the step when he was hit on the forehead with a hard, metallic object.

"Ow!"

He glared at the squirrel, then bent to pick up the object which was, of course, his gold winged horse brooch. He sighed. The squirrel, satisfied its message had been delivered, chirped and bounded across the roof toward the paddock.

He thrust the brooch into his pocket, and when he entered the cabin, he saw the hermit bent over a pot on the fire. "You need to mind your squirrels."

"*My* squirrels?" the hermit said without looking up. "They are not *my* squirrels. If they belong to anyone, it's Fyrian, a goddess your people once worshipped, but now long forgotten. She looked after woodlands and its creatures and was particularly fond of squirrels. She might have even appeared in the guise of one from time to time. But yes, they are very nosy creatures and have no qualms about getting into your business."

"That's an understatement," Tavin said with a derisive laugh.

The hermit lightly tapped his ladle on the rim of the pot. "You will want to keep your voice down, my friend. Your lieutenant has only just settled."

Tavin stepped over to her bedside. Her cheeks were a more normal pink now. She seemed to rest peacefully.

"She is a strong one," the hermit said, "and a fighter. This is good. Now come sit." He indicated a chair at the table. "I've made soup and it may hearten you." He ladled some into a bowl and placed it before Tavin.

"What is in it?"

"Good things I picked in the forest today including the Chicken of the Woods. Go ahead, try it."

Tavin was thinking squirrel might be a choice addition when the hermit's pet appeared in the window to spy on them. The soup, however, was tangy in an herby way, and the fungus actually kind of tasted like chicken and had the right texture. It made the soup plenty filling.

"Not bad," he said.

The hermit smiled and sat across from him. "A word of advice about squirrels, my friend. It's best not to throw rocks at them, even when they are being nosy busybodies. Not only is it unkind to do so, but our little friends tend to carry a grudge."

"I noticed."

The hermit watched him eat for a while before saying, "We did not finish speaking about your ability."

"I don't want it."

"Regardless of your wishes in the matter, young Tavin, you have it. Your lieutenant is showing signs of improvement, but once her memories begin to afflict her again, that tenuous improvement will diminish rapidly."

"You are saying her emotions, her memories, will kill her?"

"It happens more often than you'd guess. Despair is an insidious emotion, and at its bleakest, it is a wish for death. The desire to be with her loved one on the other side of the veil pulls at her, the release it could bring when all that is on this side is so very hard."

Tavin gazed into his empty bowl. He didn't want this terrible ability, but he didn't want the lieutenant to die either. "What do I do?"

"I will show you how to relieve her of her emotional distress, while at the same time providing her the support she needs without being intrusive. Most importantly, I will show you how to shield yourself from her emanations. Hers, and everyone else's."

Tavin sat up straight. "That's possible? To—to shield myself?"

"Yes, my friend. And you need to learn it, or you, too, are susceptible to seeking the other side."

The last slipped right past Tavin. "What about what I did to that man?"

"Yes," the hermit said, "we will go over that, too."

"When do we start?"

The hermit chuckled. "Eager now, are we? Is immediately soon enough?"

Tavin nodded.

"Good. Let us move outside where we will not disturb your lieutenant's rest."

Tavin glanced anxiously at her.

"Come now," the hermit said, "you will know if she needs help."

They sat on the ground in front of the cabin with a candle between them. Bats swooped and whirled overhead hunting for moths and biters. The hermit first taught Tavin how to form a barrier in his mind so that the emotions of others did not become mired with his own. There were different gradations of shields, the hermit told him. He could shut out everyone, or keep a minimal shield in which the emotions of others were there, but muffled.

"It is like wearing clothing, eh?" the hermit said. "You wear different layers of clothing to protect yourself from the cold or heat. The difference is, keeping a shield up can be tiresome, and that is why having a range of shield layers can be helpful."

Tavin put the analogy to use, imagining himself dressed in different layers of clothing to build his shields. It did take energy and concentration, but the imagery made it easier.

"It will become second nature with time," the hermit said. "You will change the strength of your shields without thinking. However, to help people with their emotions, you need to be somewhat open to them, allow yourself to feel what they feel. Peel back the layers."

For this, Tavin imagined himself removing mittens so he could hold the person's emotions in his hands.

"Then you will gently discharge the energies," the hermit continued, "into the earth." He pointed at a patch of dirt beside him and a tree frog hopped onto his hand. "Hello, my tiny friend." He lowered it onto some moss. "You must reverse the energy, but not back at the one creating the emotions. Gently into the earth."

"It won't do anything to, er, the earth?"

"The energy emitted is so minor, much smaller than our little frog friend, that it leaves no imprint and does no harm. Emotional energy is part of nature, too."

Tavin nodded. Fireflies blinked around them and deep into the woods like fairy lights as the hermit instructed him on how to provide calming support to a distressed person. The squirrel he called Winterberry watched from her branch and periodically offered her own pointed opinion.

"There is a give and take to it," he explained, "a flow. You receive the emotions from the distressed person and discharge them gently into the earth, and you return to the person the calm, or encouragement, or whatever it is they may need. You can create for them a state of mind that allows them to tell you how they are afflicted, allowing you to help them further."

"This really works?" Tavin asked, but before the hermit had the chance to reply, the grief in the lieutenant reawakened. He clamped down his shields right away, imagining himself in every coat and hat he owned.

"I would say the answer is yes," the hermit replied wryly.

"Now open yourself little by little so you can feel the grief at a bearable level, then pass it into the earth."

Tavin removed his metaphorical gloves and a coat or two, and accepted the lieutenant's grief, allowing it to fill his hands and the layers of himself he left unshielded. Her sorrow and yearning had distance now. It did not fill him with screaming torment. He cradled the sorrow with reverence and then turned his palms down toward the ground to discharge it.

"Well done," the hermit exclaimed.

"To think I could have saved myself so much agony had I known this long ago," Tavin said.

"But you know now and forever, and that is no small thing. However, you are not yet done."

No, he wasn't. More emotion was streaming from the lieutenant. He repeated the process, and this time the hermit reminded him to extend a sense of peace to her, to let her know she was not alone.

He reached out to her with waves of calm, connected and—

—was pulled in. He was pulled into a dark place where she stood in her slashed and bloodstained uniform in front of a full-length mirror. The mirror was cracked all over.

She murmured, "I am broken."

"Um," Tavin replied.

"I could not save them. I could not save *him*."

Tavin did not know what to say.

Reassure her, came the hermit's voice into his mind.

"I am sorry," Tavin said. "I am sorry they are gone. But you are not alone. I am here with you, and so is the hermit. And there are all the Riders back in Sacor City."

She simply stared at her shattered reflection, said nothing.

"Um . . ."

Tell her how strong she is, the hermit prompted.

"You are the strongest person I've ever met," he told her. "I used to call you the Ice Lady. Maybe I shouldn't tell you that. But anyway, now that I know you a little more, I know you were like that because you were holding everything in, but you don't have to. I can help. I—"

An avalanche of emotion filled with images of death and gore fell on him and swept away his shields. He barely heard the hermit tell him to ground it. When he remembered how to do it, it funneled through him like a torrent into the ground beneath his hands. When at last the flow waned, the hermit gripped his shoulder.

"Now, Tavin, my friend, send peace back to her."

Tavin did the best he could, sending reassurance and calm on mind waves, as he thought of them, and kept his emotional distance. To his relief, she settled into dreamless rest.

Tavin blinked at his surroundings, the dark forest. Dew dampened his clothes. Winterberry chirped from her branch, and the hermit gazed at him in concern.

"That . . . That was exhausting," Tavin said, and he passed out.

When Tavin regained consciousness, a tiny nose and whiskers twitched in his face. Winterberry squabbled at him, then leaped off his chest and scrambled up the nearest tree.

"Ah, friend Tavin," the hermit said, stepping from the cabin, "you are back with us. Your timing is excellent. I've some tea for you." He carried a couple mugs, and when Tavin managed to sit up, handed one to him. "A restful chamomile."

"How long was I out?"

"Long enough for me to boil water and steep the tea."

Tavin sipped appreciatively of the tea. The hermit had added honey to it. "I'm still exhausted."

The hermit sat again. "It is not surprising. I did not expect you to join with your lieutenant's mind so totally. Yours is a powerful gift, and I have not seen such in many long years. But also, your lieutenant has a kindred ability. It is not empathic, precisely, but she can read people, yes?"

"Truth and lies," Tavin said.

"A little more cut and dry, then. Still, her ability requires sensing the honesty of others, which draws on emotional energy to a certain degree. It may explain the strength of your contact in her mind. You must be careful, for such an intrusion may not be acceptable to many, and without discipline, you could lose yourself in the other person. However, used with care, it can be an extraordinarily helpful tool in healing someone."

"I don't think I want to do it again. Ever."

"It may help your lieutenant."

Tavin sighed and blew on his tea before sipping. Everything always came back to the lieutenant.

WANDERER

While Tavin and the hermit sat outside with their tea, fireflies settled into the hermit's hair and around his head like a sparkling headdress. Tavin tried to muffle his laughter, but ended up spilling tea on himself.

"What is so funny?" the hermit demanded. When Tavin explained, he let out an annoyed *hum*. "Really, must they go a-courting in my hair? How insensible of them."

He shook his head in an attempt to dislodge them, but it only made them blink with increased fervor, which in turn made Tavin laugh harder.

"Well, of all the nuisances." The hermit sighed. "No harm, I suppose." He rose to his feet as agile as an acrobat. "It grows late, my friend, and I should be off, me and my amorously glowing friends, but I shall return tomorrow. I will check on your lieutenant, and we will continue our discussion about your ability."

"But what if the lieutenant worsens?"

"Make sure her fever stays down and offer her water if she awakens. There is not much more we can do for her this night. It is up to her now."

It wasn't a reassuring answer, and Tavin felt a pang of fear about being left alone with the lieutenant lest her condition deteriorate or she overwhelmed him with another storm of emotions. It had been such a relief to have Abram and the hermit there to take over and handle things.

"Can you find your way in the dark?" he asked. "Maybe it would be best if you stayed the night." It was an unconvincing pretext to keep the hermit near, but he had to at least try.

"I always find my way," the hermit replied.

"Do you really have to go? It's easier with you here."

"I will not be far, young Tavin. I will be but a few steps away with the spirit of the wood, and you can seek me at the oak in need." With that he strode across the clearing and disappeared into the forest, a trail of sparkling light wafting behind him.

It was a long night. Every time the lieutenant moved or made some small noise, Tavin was on his feet to check on her. He kept himself tightly shielded to protect himself from her emotions. The fever remained, and periodically he cooled her skin with a wet cloth. When she was especially restless, he read to her from one of the books on the shelf or spoke to her of inanities, of how he used to help Granny Olsted in her garden and loved digging out the potatoes, of various customers of the Barefoot Bride who would drink too much and had to be dragged outside to the street at closing, and of fireflies flashing in the hermit's hair. His rambling seemed to soothe her, but it calmed him, as well. She muttered now and then in her dreams, but she did not become agitated or take a turn for the worse.

Finally, as the golden light of dawn seeped through the window, Tavin sank to his blankets beside the bed and was out just like that.

It seemed only moments later when he was roused by footsteps creaking on the floorboards around him. He sat up with a start.

"Good morning, young Tavin," the hermit said, peering down at him. "I have brought you some fresh bread and strawberry preserves."

Tavin scrubbed his face, feeling more than a little rough. He was sore from his fight with the brigand the day before and did not feel like he'd gotten enough sleep. Then he remembered the lieutenant.

"How is she?" he asked as he attempted to unwind himself from his blankets.

"Peaceful, I think," the hermit replied. "Still fevered, but peaceful."

Tavin clambered to his feet and looked down upon her as she slept. The rise and fall of her chest beneath her covers made him sigh in relief.

"I am going to check her over and treat her wound with more herbal paste," the hermit said. "Why don't you look after your horses while I do so. They were quite insistent about wanting food when I walked up. Then come back and we'll break our fast."

Tavin nodded, pulled on his boots, and stumbled outside, frightening a squirrel that had been sitting on the front step. It squawked and launched itself at the nearest tree. The morning fresh air cleared his head of cobwebs, even more so when he splashed cold water from the spring on his face. All the while he kept his shields firmly in place lest the lieutenant's sleep turned less peaceful.

He was replenishing the paddock trough with spring water when Abram appeared out of the woods. His demeanor was not as calm as usual. Tavin lowered his shields slightly and sensed Abram was, in fact, quite troubled.

"What is it?" Tavin asked.

The hermit poked his head out of the cabin's window. "Yes, what troubles you, Abram?"

"I tracked the brigands and gangs that have been squatting in the near woods through the night. Word has gotten out that the Red Witch is hiding somewhere in the queen's forest. Some seek vengeance for the defeat of Urz and the Darrow Raiders; others mean to make a name for themselves by capturing and killing her."

"She is safe here," the hermit said.

Abram slowly nodded. Every move he made, Tavin noticed, was deliberate as if to offset any perceptions anyone had about his size. Tavin, for one, didn't believe for a moment that there was an ounce of clumsiness in the forester. Strength and power, yes, but not clumsiness.

"That is so," Abram said, "but she cannot stay here indefinitely, and there are too many of them for me to confront on my own should they trespass upon the queen's forest. I have sent a friend with a message to Sacor City to request aid from the queen. I explained the situation."

Even if the queen sent aid, Tavin thought, he and the lieutenant could be stuck here for months, providing she in fact survived. He didn't relish the idea of having to fight his way out.

"There is not much more that can be done for now," the hermit said, "but you look as if you could use some breakfast. Will you join us?"

"My thanks for the offer," Abram replied, "but I must continue to patrol my borders. In the meantime, I advise Rider Tavin not to stray past the wards for brigands are hunting Green Riders."

Tavin shuddered. "Does that mean I shouldn't visit the hermit at the oak?"

"Using the spirit of the wood to visit the hermit remains a safe path," Abram replied, "and I will sit with the lieutenant tomorrow so you can do just that."

"Thank you, my friend," the hermit said. "You keep safe, as well."

"I will," Abram said, and without another word, he turned and strode into the forest disturbing neither fern nor branch.

"Come in for breakfast," the hermit told Tavin. "After, we will speak of what you have learned, and what you have yet to know."

Over tea and the hermit's dense and crusty bread, on which

they smeared strawberry preserves, they quietly reviewed Tavin's lessons from the previous day—how to shield himself in layers to protect himself from the emotions of others, and how to peel back the layers to accept varying levels of emotions to help someone who was suffering, how to ground those emotions, and how to return calm and support. Tavin had accidentally gone a step further and entered the lieutenant's mind.

"It takes discipline not to be swept away," the hermit said, "and someone with your ability harboring ill intent? I do not wish to think of the damage that could be done."

Tavin hadn't considered that.

"Most people who would do that," the hermit mused, "most likely lack any kind of empathy to begin with, and therefore would not receive the gift, which, I suppose, makes it a moot point, but it is still a horrifying notion to imagine. In any case, you must practice these skills you have learned so that you can use them without thinking."

Tavin nodded. "I have been keeping myself shielded since last night. I think I managed to keep them up while I was sleeping." Not that he had slept much.

"Very good. Excellent. You are a quick learner, which is a good thing with so strong an ability."

Tavin sat back in his chair with his hands clasped around his mug. He glanced at the lieutenant to ensure she still rested easily. Reassured that she did, he turned his attention back to the hermit.

"How do you know so much about my ability?"

The hermit's eyes flashed gold in the sunlight that filtered through the window. The seams of his wise but ageless face deepened as he smiled. "I know a good many things, friend Tavin. I have lived long in the world, and there was a time when magic and magic users were plentiful. Some had empathic gifts. I dwelled now and then in the lodges of the great mages learning from them and reading the scrolls and books in their libraries. The Scourge was a great crime after the Long War of your people against Mornhavon the Black. The lodges and their libraries were burned down, and those with any magical ability sacrificed to the D'Yer Wall, or executed outright."

"What? The Scourge was a disease, a plague." That was what the histories said. Disease swept through the lands disproportionately killing magic users. And the D'Yer Wall? That wasn't something he had heard mentioned in a long time, an artifact of such ancient days that it was more legend than fact and largely forgotten.

"It was a disease most certainly," the hermit replied. "A disease of mistrust and hatred. People killing their own folk out of fear of their differences."

"You know this because . . . ?"

"Because I was there. In fact, I barely escaped the anti-magic mobs with my hide intact."

"But that would make you, well, ancient."

"And so I am. I knew the great oak when it was but an acorn."

Tavin's mouth dropped open. "*Who* are you? Are you an Eletian?"

The hermit laughed. "Forgive me my mirth, my friend. I

am not an Eletian. Those folk are . . . How shall I put it? Too high above it all and enigmatic for the simple likes of me. But who am I? First and foremost, I am the hermit who lives by the great oak. I have been known by countless names over countless centuries, for I was a wanderer learning the ways of the world and its peoples, watching them rise and fall, learn again, and then lose all knowledge and sink back into primitive ways. I have seen gods and goddesses walk the Earth only to be replaced by new beliefs and deities. I fought during the great dark of the Black Ages when demons invaded the living world and sought to turn it into a hell. I watched the Kmaernians build their first stone towers, and the sea kings retreat across the ocean. I witnessed the rise of Mornhavon and the devastation he wrought."

It was incredible, a lot to take in. "So, you are . . . immortal?"

The hermit chuckled. "No, friend Tavin. Nothing lasts forever, though the Eletians are closer to immortal than I."

"Who are your people? Are you the only one?"

The hermit's expression fell and silence filled the cabin for a time before he answered. "I believe I may be the last of my kind. The Imnatar, people of the forest. The place of my birth was on a far continent. Mine were a gentle folk who subsisted on the gifts of the forest, but for some it was not enough and they sought to rule all through the use, or rather misuse, of etherea. Their selfish desire for power threw the land out of balance causing one disaster after another. After the rains stopped and the forest turned to dust, my people fled to other lands that were not so devastated. They merged with other peoples and diminished. Those who sullied the etherea in their pursuit of power seemingly vanished from existence, but really, they exist just beyond the liminal line, just outside our ken, immersed still, in the etheric." He frowned. "They think to ascend to godhood by mastering the weaving of the universe."

Tavin did not understand all that he said, but before he could ask, the hermit added, "As for me, I just kept wandering."

"I'm sorry," Tavin said, "that your people are gone."

"Sorry? No, my friend, it is the nature of things. The changes, the cycles, those who seek to take what is not theirs. It happens over and over. As for me, my life has been very rich. I have seen so much, and now that book I received from you about the Cloud Islands makes me anxious to venture forth again. Such time has elapsed that much will be new."

"I would like to hear all about your travels." Tavin thought about Granny Olsted, who had given him the book and how he had longed to leave his village in Adolind.

"It would be years in the telling, my friend."

"Maybe just some of the stories, then."

"You shall have them, but we've your lessons first. Or, perhaps, less a lesson and more a caution about the use of your ability, how you used it to kill a man."

Tavin shifted uneasily in his chair. He had not wanted to even think about it and now the image of the man writhing on the ground and pleading with him to "make it stop" came back to him all too clearly. "I—" He didn't know what to say. He was not sorry the man was dead, but at the same time, the power he had unleashed, whatever it was he had done, was unnerving.

"He was a very bad man, no doubt about it," the hermit said. "There are, unfortunately, many like him in the world. There always have been. I believe in the beauty of life, young Tavin, but sometimes to preserve life, a cancer must be cut away, eh? That man was a cancer and we are well rid of him. I am more interested in how your ability removed this cancer."

"I don't know what I did," Tavin replied. "I was upset and . . ." He shrugged.

"More than upset, I should think. You were full of the pain and grief of your lieutenant, yes? Not to mention all that you carried within you since you were a small boy."

"And the feelings of the man. He was vile." Tavin shuddered. "While we were fighting, I felt how much he loved killing, and I—I received images and memories of him and his victims. Things I never want to see again. I was disgusted, horrified. *Angry.* It all rushed out of me at once."

"You grounded all that you held within you into the man, yes?"

Tavin nodded thoughtfully. "Yes, I think that's right. Somehow I knew to ground it into him."

"A natural instinct. Your defenses were triggered. Grounding those emotions into earth is harmless, as all energies come from nature, but all of what you held discharged into another living being? A man cannot withstand it."

"So I discharged everything I had into the man," Tavin murmured. It had been awful enough that the brigand had clawed his own eyes out. "I made him experience all the

trauma he forced on his victims from their point of view. He
felt everything they had felt when he hurt them."

"A most fitting punishment, I think. You have an empathic ability that can help others like your lieutenant, but
with your strength, it is also a weapon."

Tavin sat with that for a moment. The lilting song of a
white-throated sparrow drew his gaze out the window where
insects hovered and buzzed in the golden haze of sunshine.
He had only ever known his sensitivity to the emotions of
others, how it tormented him, but within the span of a day
and a half he had learned not only how to protect himself
and help others, but how to use his ability to kill.

"I trust," the hermit said, "that I do not have to explain
the consequences and responsibilities of such power."

No, he did not. "Why didn't I feel the man's pain after I
did what I did to him."

"I do not know. Perhaps you intuitively learned to shield
yourself. Or perhaps you expended all you had to give at
that moment. You depleted your empathic ability to the extent you could no longer sense him. Even great mages had
limits to their powers. All the more reason not to overdo
when working with someone who needs your help."

"I was warned during Rider training that using one's
ability has a price. Some people get headaches, or grow very
tired. Things like that. I fainted when I killed that man. Also
when I helped the lieutenant."

"Yes. You must remember that using your ability can
leave you vulnerable, and to do so only when the circumstances are safe for you. These were both intense situations,

and perhaps when you use your ability in less powerful ways, the reaction will be less dramatic."

"I don't like passing out," Tavin said, "but if I've always had this ability, why didn't I have reactions to it before?"

"Were you using it," the hermit asked, "or just letting it flow through you?"

"I guess I was doing anything I could to avoid it."

The hermit nodded. "You were not using it, then. You also did not have that winged horse brooch, which augments your magic and may, as a result, make any reaction stronger."

Tavin sighed. At some point—he didn't remember when—he had pinned his brooch back on his shortcoat. Now he passed his fingers across its smooth, cool surface.

"Do not fear, my friend, you will, with time, have the knack of it. Now perhaps, if you are still wanting them, we will have stories of my travels."

When Tavin responded with an enthusiastic yes, the hermit launched into tales of journeys into lands now lost beneath the seas, of peoples with strange names and stranger customs, of wars forgotten in time, and of abandoned cities buried deep beneath the ground. The world was a living entity, the hermit told Tavin, and changed over millennia as any person would in their short lifetime. Such was the spell the hermit cast that Tavin felt he floated along with him down rivers, dragged himself up the highest of mountains, shared bread and wine with an affluent people on a far continent, and dwelled in the intense heat of desert lands. He could *feel* the grit of sand in his teeth, the cool relief of an oasis.

The lieutenant remained quiet throughout, perhaps kept

calm by the hermit's voice as it rose and fell with the stories he told. He had a knack for twining one narrative with another and explained that the world was not simple but a great tapestry of delicately woven threads and, therefore, stories about it should not be either. Tavin was surprised by how quickly the day passed. Already the birds sang their evensong. But now the hermit looked out the window and the lowering sun shone upon his face. He slowly blinked as if registering some message from the outside world.

"The day has grown old, my friend," he said, "and I must return home." Tavin must have looked disappointed for he added, "Abram comes to sit with your lieutenant on the morrow, and you will find me at the great oak."

The hermit checked the lieutenant over once more before he departed. Tavin, meanwhile, stepped outside to feed the horses. Gradually the gossamer threads of the tales the hermit had woven snapped and released him though he was loath to be free. Goose and Bluebird, however, had real appetites in the here and now, and they were not shy about letting him know. He shook off the last of the cobwebs, laughed, and served them their grain.

The hermit joined him outside. "I believe your lieutenant will do well enough through the night. I feel more confident the immediate danger has passed."

It was good news and Tavin was relieved.

"Now mind your shields," the hermit continued, "but do not overdo. Relax them now and again. If you sense your lieutenant in emotional distress, help her, but remember all you've learned."

"Receive the emotion and ground it in the earth," Tavin said, "and offer calm."

The hermit grinned. "Very good. You are my brightest student."

Tavin watched after the hermit as he vanished into the woods. He laughed when it occurred to him that he was the hermit's *only* student.

Upon reentering the cabin, he gazed at the lieutenant in her blissfully unaware state and sobered. He hoped she gave him no reason to have to use his ability.

THE DARKEST DARK

Tavin spent the remainder of the day collecting and chopping wood, repairing a paddock fence rail, reading, and keeping an eye on the still-sleeping lieutenant. Cautiously he lowered his shields but sensed no more from her than somnolence. He guessed the infection and fever had so exhausted her body and mind that even her nightmares had gone dormant.

As night fell, he checked on the horses one last time and brought more water from the spring into the cabin for drinking and the soothing of fevers. When he was done, he spread out his blankets between the bed and the fireplace and lay down. He hoped for an uneventful night.

It was not. At some point past midnight, he was awakened by a disturbance. It wasn't the lieutenant's emotional emanations leaking through his light shields that awakened him. Cool night air stirred across the cabin's floor. The door creaked. It stood ajar.

"What? Lieutenant?" He sat up trying to jog his groggy head to wakefulness. When he peeled away his shields, his awareness of her was more distant than it ought to have been. The glow of the fire's embers revealed the bed was empty.

"Damnation." He stumbled out of the cabin. "Lieu-tenant?"

Moon and starlight mottled the cabin clearing. All was quiet, but her desire for vengeance filled his mind; her desire to kill those who had murdered her Sam. Clumsily he received her emotions and discharged them, and attempted to send calm, while urgently trying to see where she had gone.

Eventually he found her on the edge of the clearing about to step through the wards, her bare skin alabaster in the glow of the moon, her hair gone red-gold. The blade of her saber gleamed in her hand. He blinked as though it were a dream, for she seemed fey, a mystical fairy of old tales come to life as she stood on the edge of the forest knee-deep in ferns that nodded in nocturnal air currents, clumps of moss underfoot.

His fancy did not last long, however, for her sword slipped from her fingers and she crumpled to the ground. He ran to where she lay curled amid the ferns in a pool of moonlight and gathered her into his arms. Her skin was hot with fever.

"You should not be up and about," he gently chided her.

"They killed him, they killed Sam."

Crystalline tears beaded on her cheeks, but he felt only her iron will.

"Lieutenant," he said, "you killed them, the Raiders. You killed them all."

He hadn't been a Green Rider when she led them to victory over the Darrow Raiders. He'd heard veiled comments about how that campaign had changed her, had changed them all. It seemed Queen Isen believed the Riders could do the job no one else seemed able to. He'd also heard that the final battle had not been a battle at all. The lieutenant had ordered the source of the Raiders' drinking water poisoned, and those who did not succumb to the poison were slaughtered even as they lay sick on the ground. Some might reckon poison a dishonorable act, but in the case of the Darrow Raiders, who had been nothing less than brutal as they terrorized the countryside butchering innocents and showing no honor whatsoever, the means of their defeat was unimportant. The fact they had been defeated was everything. He'd never heard anyone argue otherwise.

He carried her back into the cabin and placed her on the bed. He thought he should check her wounds, but he wanted to make sure her mind was settled. He found her brow to still be overly warm, but she hadn't the raging fever of before.

"How about some water?" he asked.

"Yes, water," she murmured.

He lit a candle so he could see better, then helped her drink a bit. After, he cooled her skin with a wet cloth.

She settled back into her pillow, her sheets drawn to her chin. "We got them? We got them all?"

"Yes," he said, "they are all gone." He sensed her satisfaction as she drifted into sleep.

He sank into his own blankets and remembered to ground what had been projected into him, and he, too, finally slept.

In the dream, he was in the common room of the Barefoot Bride. His uncle was raging at him as usual, but about what, he knew not. The laughter and conversation of the customers were deafening. It hurt his head. He raged back at his uncle. "I'm leaving! Then see how you get on." He rushed to his room and started packing a sack with his few belongings. He kept packing and packing, but his belongings proliferated and there was no end to the things he must stuff into his sack. He couldn't leave until he had everything. Suddenly his sack tumbled over and spilled out the contents—thousands of acorns. *Oh, no!* He dove to the floor and started collecting them to stuff back into his sack, but they, too, multiplied.

"We used to play cards."

He looked up. Seated on the side of his dream bed was the lieutenant. She gazed at a mirror. He'd seen it before. All the fractures on the surface remained. Or, maybe not all. Some fine cracks were gone.

"Cards?" he asked.

"We'd gamble." She chuckled, but her gaze did not waver from her distorted reflection. "We'd gamble with hard candies we'd get from Master Gruntler's."

The candy maker in Sacor City. "Who did you play cards with?"

"Sam," she said, and though her voice had not changed, he felt her answer as a lament.

"Who won?"

"I did, usually. Especially at Knights. He played only to humor me, and called me a wicked gambler." A wan smile flickered across her face.

An image flashed into his mind of a man sitting across a

table laying down his cards. He was a handsome fellow as far as Tavin could judge such things, with a firm chin, black hair, and startling blue eyes.

"We'd made plans to marry when my time with the Riders ended," she continued. "We'd go home to Penburn. I was going to teach him how to handle a boat on the river. We had so many plans."

The setting of his dream washed away and immersed them in the dark place. He could see only her gazing into the fractured mirror. He realized he was no longer asleep, but in her mind.

"The Raiders came," she said, "and that changed everything."

He was blasted with images of the Green Riders placed on a war footing with hard training and discipline drilled into them. Sabers sharpened. Grim determination on their faces as they hunted down Darrow Raiders. All followed by the horror committed upon them by the enemy, the fierce battles, the torture and desecration.

Tavin caught himself screaming. He slammed his hand onto the floorboards to discharge the dark and grisly scenes she replayed in her mind.

"The Darrow Raiders are done," he told her over and over. "You defeated them." But had she really if her memory of them still tormented her so?

"My friends are gone," she said, "and my Sam."

Another crack etched itself into the mirror.

"No, no, no," Tavin muttered. But then, weirdly, an acorn

dropped on his head and bounced to the floor. "Ow! Dammit!" Acorns reminded him of the hermit and that he had to do more.

He suffused his presence in her mind with warmth and comfort. "Your experiences were terrible," he told her. "No one should have to go through all that."

She turned to look into the dark. "I want to be with him. I am empty without him."

This was not good. She was sliding back into darkness. The darkest dark. "I can understand that," he said hastily. "But would he want that for you? Wouldn't he wish for you to live on and be happy? And what of those whom you leave behind? We need you. We understand, but we don't want you to leave. If you stay, you won't be alone. *You are not alone.*" He grasped for anything that came to mind. "Prince Zachary would be especially sad to see you go."

Her shoulders sagged, and she looked down at her feet. "Oh, Zachary. Such a serious boy."

Tavin knew little of her connection to the young prince, just that they were friends, she like a big sister to him. He had, at least, finally caught her attention. "Many love you. You can lean on them. I am here. You are not alone."

She turned to him, and as if suddenly aware of his presence, demanded, "Who are you?"

The question startled him. "It's me, Tavin. The Rider you are training." Had she not realized all along to whom she'd been speaking? Perhaps to her it was all a dream.

"Tavin. I remember. But you don't know me. Not really."

"That is true, but I am getting to know you little by little.

I know you like wild blueberries, and now I know you like Master Gruntler's hard candies. I am here, and you are not alone. Your grief is deep, and your friends and I will support you. Bluebird will, too." He tried to send her more reassurance and warmth.

"All right," she said, and that was all.

Tavin gasped when he was shunted from her mind, and this time he did pass out.

Voices.

Voices and a stone in the small of his back.

"—should drink more broth." A low, rumbling voice. Abram, the forester.

A faint demurral. The lieutenant.

Tavin groaned and opened his eyes to daylight. Fresh air and birdsong flowed through the open door. He rolled to his side and rubbed the small of his back, then felt around for the stone that caused him such discomfort. It turned out to be an acorn.

"Five hells."

"Good morning, Rider Tavin," Abram said.

Tavin gazed blearily up at the big man who sat at the table with his pipe. "Morning."

"There are oats and hot water for tea on the fire when you are ready."

"The lieutenant?"

"See for yourself."

Tavin climbed to his feet and cloaked himself in a light shield. He looked down upon the lieutenant, who gazed back at him with intent hazel eyes.

He smiled tentatively. "It's good to see you awake."

"Who is tending the horses?" Her voice rang strong and sharp, and it took him by surprise.

"I'm sorry, I—"

"Never fear," Abram said in his slow, calm baritone. "I took care of them. Young Tavin here no doubt needed the rest."

"They need more than feeding and water," she said. "Have they been getting any exercise? Is the paddock clean? Horse before Rider."

Horse before Rider was drilled into every green Greenie during training. He hadn't meant to oversleep, but the use of his ability had clearly left him exhausted.

"I'll go check on them now," he said, "and clean the paddock." He grabbed his boots and shortcoat.

As he stepped outside, he heard Abram say, "Riding in the forest is not safe just now, and I could not wake the lad earlier. It was not a normal sleep."

"Our horses are everything," the lieutenant said. "It's his duty to—"

Tavin snapped his strongest shields into place and hurried to the paddock not wanting to hear more, stung as he was by her tone. He thought that after everything, how he'd tried to help her during the night, that she'd at least be thankful for all he'd done on her behalf, and that maybe the Ice Lady had melted. He was wrong.

He patted Goose's soft nose. People always disappointed him. He envied Abram and the hermit for being able to live alone out in the woods with only the wildlife for company.

A squirrel chittered at him from a fence post.

All right, maybe some of the wildlife could be as irritating as people.

"Winterberry," he said, "did you drop an acorn on me during the night?"

The squirrel did not answer, but hopped away as if she were also disappointed in people.

Goose nudged his shoulder and gazed at him with a big brown eye.

"I know what you want," Tavin said. He scratched the gelding's neck. Goose leaned into it and sighed. "Yes, horses are better than people." Squirrels, on the other hand, not so much, but he dared not say it aloud.

ACORN AND HONEYCOMB

Just as Tavin finished shoveling out manure from the paddock, Abram came out and handed him a bowl of oats and
a mug of steaming tea. The forester then leaned against the
fence, aromatic smoke drifting from his pipe. Tavin ate his
breakfast eagerly.

"Laren is fast asleep, lad," Abram said. "You'll be wanting to go see the hermit. While you are gone, I will sit with
Laren and talk to these fine fellows to pass the time." He
patted Bluebird's neck. Winterberry shrieked and chattered.
"And to the squirrel," he amended.

Tavin gave his empty bowl and mug back to Abram and
grabbed his shortcoat from where he had draped it over the
fence while he worked. "Do I have to do the sensing of the
spirit of the wood thing again?"

"That is how you find the hermit. But remember, do not
go beyond the wards to do so. Too dangerous."

"But I'll have to pass through the wards into the forest to
reach the great oak," Tavin said.

"Yes, but that path will be safe."

Tavin shook his head. He'd say it was all nonsense if he hadn't already found his way to the great oak the first time.

He sat on a stump near the wards and tried to ignore the sounds of the horses in the paddock, of the cabin door creaking and shutting as Abram went inside. He tried to open his mind to the forest. He had an itch behind his ear. A biter buzzed around his head that he had to wave away. His mind wandered to the lieutenant's sharp words earlier, such a contrast to her underlying emotions and vulnerability. Settling down was not easy.

Finally, he closed his eyes and let go a deep breath. He listened to the forest sounds, especially the restive breeze among the trees. It was like the forest was breathing as he breathed. The shade kept him cool and ferns rustled around him, and the pleasant scents of balsam fir and sweet fern baking in patches of sunlight drifted to him.

When he opened his eyes, a gently trod path lay before him. He stood and stepped onto it. The cabin and paddock still lay behind him. Goose nickered.

"I'll be back soon," Tavin told him.

With but a few strides, however, the waystation vanished and the edge of the glade of the great oak appeared before him. A commotion greeted him—birds fluttered to and fro among the branches and in the air, squirrels were in a furor shrieking and darting, a cloud of bees swarmed around the great oak, and the hermit stood with his hands on his hips face-to-face with a bear.

"I warned you," the hermit admonished the bear. "But did you listen? No, of course not."

The bear groaned and swiped at bees buzzing around its face.

"Go on, be off with you." The hermit made shooing motions, and the bear jogged from the glade into the woods. A dark flume of angry bees billowed after it. "Friend Tavin!" the hermit called. "As you see, we've had some excitement this morning. Bear thought he could help himself to some honeycomb in the oak, and now I must restore the queen to her throne so the hive will settle down."

Tavin, wary of being stung, kept his distance and watched the hermit, seemingly oblivious to the anger of the bees, lean halfway into the crack in the oak's trunk and presumably search for the queen.

"Where are you, Your Majesty?" came his muffled voice. "Your court is in need of you. Lots of drones, lots of drones, more drones, uh—ah ha! I see you!"

A moment later, the hermit emerged with a look of triumph on his face. "The bear broke their hive to get at the honey, of course. It was only a small section, thankfully, so I've restored the queen to her throne in the undamaged part. Now to help the others find her."

The hermit looked at the oak's trunk, and Tavin realized it was alive with masses of milling bees. The hermit scooped them up by the handful and passed them through the tree's crack. He repeated the process several times until the rest seemed to get the idea and moved themselves. The hermit, Tavin thought, was made of much sterner stuff than he.

When the hermit finished, he carried out two chunks of

dripping honeycomb. "These the bear broke, and no sense of letting it go to waste."

Tavin gladly accepted his unexpected treat. Sticky golden ambrosia smeared his chin and oozed down his shirt as he held the honeycomb over his tongue to get every last drop.

"I have some other pieces dripping into a jar for you to take to the waystation," the hermit said, his face gleaming with a glaze of honey.

Tavin was not displeased. After they washed up and drank from the nearby stream, he asked, "Didn't the bees sting you?"

"Nah. They knew I was trying to help, not hurt them. They'd have sacrificed themselves for nothing since they die when they sting someone."

Tavin still was not anxious to try carrying handfuls of bees like the hermit had. They found a place to sit beneath the oak.

"You found the way this time without the help of the squirrels, eh?" the hermit asked as old Raincloud climbed up his arm to drape around his neck.

"Yes," Tavin replied. In the excitement with the bear, and then the intoxicating surprise of the treat of honey, he had forgotten the feat. "I listened to the forest breathing."

"Ah. Perhaps you will soon hear its heartbeat. This is very good. But let us now turn to business. How fares your lieutenant?"

"She was awake this morning, and was her old, cold self." He explained how during the night his dream merged with her mind and how he tried to help her, and how different that Laren Mapstone was from the one who had greeted him in the morning.

"You did well trying to help her," the hermit said, absently petting Raincloud. "She did not go deeper into darkness. She awoke this morning, a very positive development. Yes, that is well done. As for the difference in her attitude, well, it is very possible she has no memory of you in her mind and does not recognize that part of you. I find it more likely, however, that it is her armor, that she is unaccustomed to accepting help and intimacy, and certainly cannot stand being so emotionally and physically vulnerable. And here you got to see her deepest self exposed. So, when she was awake and in control of herself, she clad herself in her armor as self-protection."

"I almost feel like I don't want to help her anymore," Tavin said, "if that's the thanks I get."

"I understand, my friend, but she may not see it as help but interference, or even an attack. But do not be daunted. She may not understand now, but she will one day, and that it is not just aid you are giving her, but an intrinsic part of yourself. Besides, you aren't doing this just for her gratitude, are you?"

"I suppose not." Tavin understood it was not easy for her, but it wasn't easy for him either.

"Let us work on firming up your shielding," the hermit said, "so you can sleep the night without her emotions leaking into your dreams, yet allowing you to remain attuned to her lest she decline again and require help."

They did so and the afternoon passed pleasantly. They ate raspberries plucked from brambles on the glade's edge, soaked in the sunshine, and laughed when a luna moth landed on the hermit's nose and stayed there for several minutes. At the end of the afternoon, the hermit gave Tavin two stoneware jars, one filled with honey, the other with fresh medicinal paste to daub on the lieutenant's wounds.

"I will be over tomorrow to check on her progress," the hermit said.

Tavin said his goodbyes and within a few steps was once more in the waystation clearing. When he looked over his shoulder, the path to the great oak had vanished. It was very strange, but it was a relief to know the oak was not far away so long as he was able to sense the spirit of the wood.

Light glancing off a metallic object at the edge of the clearing caught his eye. When he went to find the source of the reflection, he discovered it was the lieutenant's saber. She had dropped it in the night just before she collapsed. He'd forgotten about it after carrying her back into the cabin. So much of that had felt like a dream. He tugged it out of the tangle of underbrush and took it up to the cabin.

Inside, Abram was helping the lieutenant to sip water. "Welcome back. You had a good day with the hermit?"

"Very good, and I have fresh honey," Tavin replied. He set the jars on the table, then took out a handkerchief to wipe down the saber.

"Is that my sword?" the lieutenant asked in a tired voice.

"Yes," Tavin replied. "I found it where you dropped it last night."

She closed her eyes and leaned back into her pillow. Her cheeks turned rosy. "I had thought that all a dream. I dreamed I was going to go kill Urz and Torq, and then I realized I was . . ." The pink of her cheeks deepened to red.

She had realized she was naked, he thought. Vulnerable in more ways than one.

"You were about to step through the wards when I found you," Tavin said, "but you collapsed first." He sheathed the sword and placed it beside the bed where he had stowed her gear.

"So many dreams," she murmured, and she seemed to recede.

"Well, now, Rider Tavin," Abram said, "it was time I returned to my work. I will not be able to visit tomorrow."

"The hermit said he would come here."

"Very good." Abram took him aside and quietly said, "Your lieutenant has slept a good deal, but is not much fevered, and more accepting of broth, and even a little solid food. We can hope she'll recover her strength quickly."

Tavin hoped she would, except it also meant that they'd have to leave the forest behind sooner and he'd once more have to live in the city with all those people and the turmoil and tumult of their emotions.

SQUIRRELS

"I can do it myself."

"Yes, Lieutenant." Tavin handed her the jar of healing paste. Night had fallen and she'd needed a fresh application before bedtime.

When she gave him a pointed look, he knew to turn away so she could smear the paste on without an audience.

"Isn't like I haven't seen everything already." Just thinking about it, however, made his cheeks heat up.

She did not reply, but made a weak grunt of effort. When the sound turned into a groan of pain, he muttered, "Sake of the gods," and spun around. She was attempting to rub the paste onto the wound in her belly area with a shaking hand.

"*Rider,*" she snapped.

"I think at this point you can just call me Tavin." He knelt beside the bed and gently took the jar from her hand. She'd made a mess, but the healing paste on her healthy skin wouldn't hurt anything so he left it. With a delicate touch he daubed the paste on her wounds, all the way from her chin, down her neck and torso, to her hip. It was a gruesome wound and appeared worse in some ways as it began to heal than it had when it was fresh. His terrible stitches made it look all the more ghastly. She sagged into the mattress as though exhausted by the mere effort of having tried to do it herself. Tears leaked from the corners of her eyes.

"Am I hurting you?" he asked. He was keeping himself tightly shielded to repel her emotions.

"No," she whispered.

He suspected if he had *her* special ability, it would be informing him she had lied.

"Almost done." He hoped telling her that would help not only with the discomfort but the modesty issue. He smeared more paste on the wound beneath her rib cage.

"So weak," she murmured. "Weaker than a baby."

Ah, he thought, that was probably bothering her far more than the pain or her nakedness.

"It will pass. You have been through a lot."

By the time he finished, she had fallen asleep. He pulled the covers up and rested his wrist against her cheek and forehead to ensure the fever was under control. She was warm, but not terrible, and he sighed in relief.

He sank to his own blankets on the floor beside the bed and gazed into the embers of the fire. If their roles had been reversed, he was fairly sure she'd care for him as he did for her. The Green Riders were a tight-knit group that looked out for one another, or at least, that was what he'd been told. He'd kept to himself too much in order to avoid the hail of emotions that hammered him whenever he was around the exuberant Riders, which prevented him from experiencing the camaraderie of being one of them. Now, thanks to the hermit's lessons, he had some hope of being able to join in with excursions to Sacor City's taverns and getting to know his fellow Riders better.

With that thought, he tightened his shields as the hermit had taught him so the lieutenant's dreams and emotions would not bleed into his, yet leave him open enough should she need him.

Tavin awoke with a start, confused at first as to where he was and what had awakened him. The lieutenant screamed. He crawled out of his blankets and rose to the side of her bed.

"Lieutenant?" He shook her. "You're having a nightmare."

"Wha—?"

"It's a nightmare," he said.

"Gods," she murmured. She drew her hand across her eyes.

"Would you like some water?"

She nodded.

He poured her a cup, then tried to help her sit up, but she batted his hands away.

"I can do it."

She struggled, and pain crossed her features, but he did not interfere. When she finally settled into a sitting position, covers drawn up over her chest, he handed her the cup.

"Thanks."

"How are you feeling?" he asked.

"Like I've been sawed down the middle and have been having constant nightmares."

"Accurate," he replied. She had left off the *How do you think I feel?* part, but he felt it right through his shields. She must be improving if she was getting even a little testy. Thanks to his shields, however, he was spared the worst.

"Can I get you more water? Tea?" he asked. "Anything I can do for you?"

She passed him the cup. "No, unless you can truly heal me."

"Sorry, no."

She closed her eyes and seemed to sink into herself, so he returned to his own bedding.

"Tavin," she said, "I've had dreams where you appear. Not tonight, but other times. We haven't discussed your new ability, though that strange mender fellow mentioned it to me. That it's an empathic ability. I don't remember what the dreams were about, just that you were there. Have you . . . Have you been in my head?"

"Yes," he replied, "but not intentionally. I—"

"Don't ever do it again," she said, her voice like a scythe out of the dark. "Don't ever get in my head again."

And that was all. Tavin lay there staring into the shadowed rafters above. Stung and upset that he always seemed to be on the wrong end of people's anger, it was a long time before he fell asleep.

In the morning, he tried to help the lieutenant get a drink of water, but she insisted on doing it herself and spilled it out of her shaky hand. He brought her some broth, and she complained it was not warm enough. When she needed to use the chamber pot, she told him to leave. He would not leave because she was too weak yet, until she made it an order.

He stood outside on the front step, taking deep breaths. A fresh cool breeze full of forest scents flowed over him, calmed him. He stood unmoving with eyes closed, drinking in the morning.

He gave the lieutenant what he guessed was a good amount of time before squaring his shoulders and entering the cabin to make sure she was all right. He found her sitting on the bed with a defiant look on her face. Not only had she managed to use the chamber pot on her own, but she'd found an oversized uniform shirt in the supply closet to wear like a nightshirt. Her expression challenged him to admonish her for overdoing.

"Well, then," he said, "if you aren't needing me for anything, I'll see to the horses."

Her expression fell as he turned to leave, as if she were disappointed he hadn't taken the bait. When he returned after feeding the horses, he found her deeply asleep. It was not the troubled slumber of one who was fevered or gripped by nightmares, but a peaceful, healing sleep, her softly freckled features free of care and her hair spread across her pillow. So innocent she looked that if he had not known her, he wouldn't have guessed her to be the sharp-tongued lieutenant that she was.

It was a different story when she woke up. This time her broth was too hot and her tea too cool. Was he taking proper care of the horses? She yelled when she spied Winterberry

sitting on the mantel. Tavin did not know how the squirrel
had entered the cabin, but she was tiny and clever. Winterberry chattered at the lieutenant.

"Get it out," the lieutenant ordered him.

As he attempted to shoo the squirrel out, Winterberry
shrieked and zipped around the cabin. She launched herself
right across the lieutenant's legs. Pots rattled and supplies
fell off shelves. He barely rescued the jar of honey the hermit
had given him. The lieutenant yelled at him and the squirrel.
She flung her cup at Winterberry, which only upset Winterberry further.

"Throwing things at squirrels—" he began.

"Get it out!"

Finally, when he opened the door, Winterberry bolted out
from beneath the bed, only to turn on the threshold, her bottle
brush tail erect, to give the lieutenant the Squirrelish equiv-
alent of a severe tongue lashing. He threw the door shut.

"I'm afraid you've made an enemy of that one," he told
the lieutenant.

"Squirrels are vermin," she replied. "Very destructive, and
the menders say they can carry disease. They are tree rats."

He sincerely hoped Winterberry was not eavesdropping.

Later that afternoon, the hermit dropped by. He checked
on the sleeping lieutenant before sitting in front of the cabin
with Tavin.

"She is improving, I think," the hermit said.

Tavin rolled his eyes. "She threw a cup at Winterberry."

"Why do you Riders insist upon throwing things at squirrels?"

"If I were feeling clever," Tavin replied, "I'd say that I've had enough acorns and spruce cones dropped on my head that maybe the squirrels deserve it." Then he sighed. "She was in quite a state—the lieutenant, not Winterberry. Actually, both of them, but I'm talking about the lieutenant." He described the scene in the cabin, the lieutenant ordering him about and issuing complaints, and most importantly, how she told him to stay out of her head. "I was only trying to help."

"Hum." The hermit scratched behind his ear, then looked at his finger upon which a spider perched. He lowered it to a nearby fern frond onto which it crawled. "She *is* getting better if she is using her energy in that manner. At least in some ways, but perhaps not others. Are the nightmares the same?"

"I don't know what she dreamed last night. I kept myself shielded, but I woke up when she screamed, and then woke her up so it would stop."

"She needs the mending of her mind," the hermit mused, "but she has told you to keep out."

"Not just told me," Tavin replied. "She ordered me to stay out."

"A dilemma. You could help her if she would allow you to join with her mind, but since she has ordered you not to, doing so would be a trespass. Unethical."

"She doesn't want help," Tavin said.

"Are you so sure, my friend?" The hermit scratched behind his ear again but, much to Tavin's relief, did not produce another spider.

"An order is pretty explicit."

"That is different from what she *needs*. Perhaps the answer is to address it head on. Use persuasion."

Tavin grimaced. He did not want to. As badly as he felt about the lieutenant's terrible past, he was content to keep his shields up and mind his own business.

The hermit sprang to his feet. "You will try persuasion, and tomorrow Abram will sit with her. You will come to the oak."

The hermit waved and departed. Tavin groaned and placed his head in his hands. He could only imagine how well addressing the lieutenant directly about joining her mind would go over.

INTO THE OAK

It did not go well.

After all of the day's activity, the lieutenant had slept deep into the night without waking. She was fevered, but only mildly. She muttered and tossed some, but did not appear to be in distress, so Tavin left her alone and settled into his bedroll.

It was dawn when the screams came.

They were now familiar screams of, he assumed, a woman seeing the mutilated remains of her lover.

He crawled to her bedside on his knees and shook her. "Lieutenant, Lieutenant, wake up. It's a dream."

Eventually he got her to wake up. Tears glinted in the morning gloom as they streamed down her cheeks. He placed a cup of water in her hands but they trembled so badly he had to help her sip. He did not think it was weakness this time that made her shake.

"Was it the dream with the mule again?" he asked.

"Were you in my head?" she demanded.

"No, Lieutenant."

She nodded and released a rattling sigh.

Then he remembered what the hermit had said the previous day. "Lieutenant, if you did let me in, I could help. I—"

"*No!*" Her tone was a dagger of jagged ice thrust into him.

"At the very least I could help you rest. These nightmares won't help you heal."

"*No.*" She was so very cold, but Tavin decided he would not be cowed.

"Check your own ability to know the truth of my words."

"Rider, I am ordering you to—"

"You are not fit to give orders," Tavin said, "and I'm not talking about your knife wound." So much, he thought, for the persuasion the hermit had advised him to use.

She quickly covered her expression of shock at his rebuttal with one of anger. "Rider, I'm warning you that you—"

"Warning me about what? That I'm being insubordinate? That you're going to put me on laundry duty once we return to Sacor City?" An image of his uncle red-faced in a rage came to him. "Maybe you plan to lash me with my belt?"

"*What?* Rider!"

"Go ahead, I've had worse, but torturing yourself over and over about the past makes you unfit. I can see it, how it makes you brittle and dark, and it will only get worse. That mirror in your dreams will keep cracking, and I will go to the captain, even the queen if I must, to have you removed from duty. You are wallowing in self-pity and making everyone else live in your shadows to such an extent that you will never heal. You won't accept help because you think it makes you weak, but there is another reason. You *want* to keep the wound raw to punish yourself, to keep reliving the horror of your past. The news is, Lieutenant, you can't change the past. There is only now and the future."

He was breathless after releasing his avalanche of words, an avalanche that had been building far longer than he had known her. An avalanche built of his years as a lonely boy buffeted by all the emotions of others and never understanding why, and never being helped, only isolated and ridiculed.

Her face had gone white, and there were many ways in which she could make his life miserable for his defiant words once they returned to Sacor City. But when had his life not been miserable?

"Get. Out." It was so softly said he almost missed it.

"Fine." He grabbed his boots and shortcoat, but paused in the doorway. The early morning light cast her as gray as a stone statue. "You aren't the only one with bad memories. You're not the only one who wishes they were dead at times." He then slammed the door and stood on the front step breathing hard.

A while later when he groomed the horses, it was with extra intensity. Neither Goose nor Bluebird complained, but rather seemed to enjoy the hard strokes of the curry comb. Afterward, he returned to the cabin's step to sit. He did not enter or even crack the door open to check on the lieutenant. She had ordered him out and that was that. He chewed on a piece of dried meat from his pack, part of his travel rations. It wasn't the best breakfast and he missed his morning tea, but he'd live. *She* could starve for all he cared.

The sun shone golden among the treetops and glistened on dew-laden cobwebs strewn across the ground by the time

Abram entered the waystation's clearing. Truth be told, he looked weary, his shoulders sagging, and with swollen pouches beneath his eyes.

"Ah, good morning, Rider," the forester said, more subdued than usual. "You are about early today."

Tavin stood. "I am. You look like you could use a few more hours of sleep, yourself."

"I've had none at all. Chasing those cutthroats out of the queen's grove all night."

"Does this mean you can't sit with the lieutenant today?"

"Quite the contrary. I will sleep when she sleeps. I have looked forward to a restful day."

"Well, she's been awake a little more often."

"That is very good news."

Tavin made a noncommittal noise.

"What is it, Rider? What's wrong?" Abram did not miss much.

"Nothing to worry about. I'll go to the hermit's now."

"Not even staying for breakfast?"

Tavin shook his head. "I already ate."

He left the bemused forester by the front step and went to the edge of the clearing to open his mind to the spirit of the wood.

The hermit was standing on his head beneath the oak when Tavin arrived.

"Friend Tavin," he called, "come join me."

"What are you doing?" Tavin asked.

"I find it most helpful to look at the world from a different perspective sometimes. Come, come try it."

Tavin was not exactly thrilled by the idea of doing a headstand. It was something he'd never been very good at. "Well, I'd rather not if you don't mind."

"But I do mind," the hermit replied. Standing on his head had no effect on his energy or enthusiasm. "Just give it a try."

Perhaps this was to be one of the hermit's lessons. It certainly sounded like it. So, with a few false starts, Tavin managed to get himself into a wobbly headstand.

"Let your weight and your being flow into your center, your core," the hermit instructed. "Steady, steady . . ."

Tavin listened and managed some form of balance. "Now what?"

"I like to quiet myself, meditate, and see how interesting the world looks upside down."

At the moment, Tavin saw only an upside-down squirrel right in front of his nose gazing at him. He wasn't sure if it was Winterberry, Sunshine, or some other. The squirrel made an inquiring chirp and tilted its head as if trying to see him right side up.

"Just listen to the leaves rustle," the hermit said. "And take in the sky. It looks like much needed rain is finally on its way."

Tavin could not hear the leaves rustle with all the blood roaring in his ears. Suddenly his leg twitched causing him to wobble. He attempted to correct his balance, but only overbalanced himself and came crashing down. The squirrel squawked and dashed off. He rolled onto his back and gazed up at the sky peeking through the leaves of the oak. Rain? The sky was blue and fair.

The hermit, who had effortlessly maintained his headstand, gracefully lowered his legs and rolled into a sitting position. The large gray squirrel, Raincloud, trundled over from the oak to climb up on the hermit's shoulders to nap.

"You did very well, friend Tavin," the hermit said. "Keep at it and you will get better and better, and be able to hold the position longer. Like you have done keeping your shields up to protect your mind. But you must not do it to the point that you close everyone out."

Tavin narrowed his eyes. That was some transition to discussing his empathic ability.

The hermit smiled innocently. "So tell me, how is your lieutenant today?"

Tavin sighed and told him everything. Afterward, the hermit shook his head.

"Stubborn Green Riders, and yes, I've encountered a few during my lifetime. You must keep trying, young Tavin. Draw down the burden she carries, or she will drown in it."

"Isn't there some other way?"

"She could live with it, the burden, at its full weight, but the question is, will that allow her to remain an adequate leader in troubled times to come? From what you told me, you certainly questioned her fitness to her face."

"Troubled times?" Tavin asked.

"Or, will she resort to other methods to blunt the trauma she's experienced? For instance, drinking intemperate quantities of alcohol to forget, or to help her sleep, or to ease the pain. Using your ability to help her would not eliminate her memories of past events, or nullify her emotions related to them, but it would lighten the load, give her space and peace to cope and move on in the world."

"Hard to do when she wants no part of it," Tavin muttered.

"Yes, as I said, stubborn Green Riders. But come with me into the oak, my friend, and perhaps you will see some things that are interesting."

Did he say *into?* Tavin followed him to the crack in the oak's trunk, the owl watching him from its burrow above. The hermit slipped into the tree.

"Come, my friend."

"I can't fit through."

"You will. The oak will permit it."

The oak would permit it? "What about the bees?"

The hermit chuckled. "They will not bother you unless you blunder into their hive like a clumsy bear."

"All right," Tavin said with a voice full of doubt. What was the worst that could happen? Probably getting caught in the crack because he couldn't fit.

He held his breath and squeezed through. Only, he needn't have for he but brushed the edges and entered easily. When he stood inside, the hollow trunk was much bigger than it had appeared from the outside—much, much bigger, and it was all gold.

THE HERMIT'S MIRROR

Tavin's eyes were dazzled by golden beams of sunlight pouring down between the branches and emerald leaves above. It was as though he had been reduced to the size of an ant for the girth and height of the trunk's hollow had enlarged so significantly. But the birds flittering in and out of the sunbeams were the usual size. Nearby, the beehive hummed. The comb flowed down the inside of the trunk like a waterfall.

The hermit chuckled. "Wondrous, is it not? A true embodiment of the spirit of the wood."

"So this is it. *This* is the spirit of the wood."

"Not precisely, my friend. The spirit of the wood is not one single thing or place. It encompasses the forest as a whole, the trees, the plants, and all the creatures to the very smallest life. It was greatest when etherea filled the world, but pockets remain within the Green Cloak, and here within the bole of the great oak is an artifact of that time."

"All the Green Cloak was like this before the Scourge?"

"Not exactly," the hermit replied. "The Scourge was indeed a major blow to etherea in the world, but even before then people made use of etherea, and when mages used it in war, there were, shall we say, droughts. Etherea is of nature, and like water it can be overused, depleted, or sullied as happened in the land of my birth. No, I speak of a time before even the Black Ages when people were few and the forest primeval. This golden light fell upon the world, but over the Ages, it has been eroded away. Let us sit for a time."

Tavin followed the hermit to where two rustic chairs made of branches waited with a table between them. Old acorns and dead leaves crunched underfoot. A few biters buzzed around his ears. These things were so ordinary amidst extraordinary surroundings.

The hermit went to a cabinet just beyond the table and pulled out his antler headdress, and placed it on his head. He sat across from Tavin, and Raincloud yawned and snuggled in closer around his neck.

"It is safe to lower your shields here," the hermit said. "Let the peace flow over you."

Tavin realized he'd become so accustomed to keeping up his shields to protect himself from the lieutenant's tempestuous emotions that he had forgotten to lower them when he arrived at the great oak. He did so now, and it was an easing of tension, like relaxing muscles that had been taut and holding up a great weight for far too long.

The golden sunshine streamed over his head and shoulders, warming him pleasantly. But it was more than warming. It was as if it flowed through his veins, tingling throughout his body. He closed his eyes. It was so peaceful, and he became sensitive to everything about the great oak, the squirrels rushing about the limbs and collecting acorns, birds resting or flirting on far branches, salamanders burrowing beneath damp and decomposing leaves; he felt the roots sipping water from deep aquifers. The taproot plunged to abyssal depths, holding the ancient tree at anchor even in the worst of storms. Through the roots, he could sense all the Green Cloak like a vast orchestra of ruffling leaves, swaying, creaking trunks, supporting myriad creatures beneath the sea of the sky. All was harmonious, all was joy, and a golden tear spilled down his cheek.

He did not know how long he sat thus, feeling himself a young sapling attuned to the spirit of the wood, when the hermit gently spoke.

"You feel it truly, eh, young Tavin? How strong it is here? Not all is well in the forest, for the lumberjacks are ever greedy for more wood, but the forest has a strong will to survive. One day humankind will be barely a memory, but the forest will continue in one form or another. I find it a deeply comforting thought."

Tavin found that he did, too. Humanity—greedy, violent, and cruel—was but a mote of dust in the scheme of nature. Individual trees may fall, even whole swaths of forest, but it would outlive people.

"There is one more thing," the hermit said. "I think you should look into my mirror."

"What? Your mirror?" The comment jolted Tavin out of his serene ruminations.

The hermit polished a shard of a mirror with the corner

of his shirt. Light glanced off it and momentarily blinded Tavin. The shard was not flat, but curved as though it was once part of a larger, convex object, a bowl, perhaps.

"Not just a simple mirror," the hermit said. "I think it may help you understand why your lieutenant could use your help, and why you must urge her to accept it."

Tavin felt a tinge of annoyance. Why did he have to worry about the lieutenant just now when he'd been basking in such peacefulness? She did not want his help, and that was that.

The hermit passed him the shard. "You have but to look into the reflection to see what you will see."

Tavin, still annoyed, held the edges of it as he had seen the hermit do to avoid smudging it with fingerprints. Carefully he turned it over to see that the concave side was also shiny and reflective.

"No, no." The hermit hastily took it from him, flipped it over, and gave it back. "Look only on this side."

The hells? Tavin thought, but he obeyed and gazed at his reflection, wondering what staring at himself would reveal. Well, he saw a distorted version of himself, thanks to the curving shape of the shard, and that he was haggard looking. He'd a bit of a scruffy beard growing. Everything else about his features, he thought, looked normal, though there was a golden haze around him.

But then the image darkened and he reappeared. No, not him, but someone who looked remarkably like him. The young man in the image suddenly crouched and covered his ears as if to protect himself from a loud noise.

Or from feeling the emotions of others.

Tavin knew that posture, that reaction, all too well. The need to protect himself but not having the knowledge of how to do so.

The image flickered again, and the man seemed to gaze back at him, this time the lines of middle age and weariness creased his features. He looked beaten down, like he had given up. He shifted, and a noose hung from a beam behind him.

The scene shimmered away, revealing a cairn grave marked with a board. Upon it was carved the name Eli Vilton. Tavin's grandfather. He'd dim memories of meeting the man who kept to himself largely like, Tavin now realized, a hermit. He had died in middle age, and Tavin's parents would not speak of him. There'd been hushed whispers about Eli around town as Tavin grew up. He tried to ignore them. They came back to him now, the rumors that Eli had killed himself.

At last it dawned on him that his grandfather had also possessed an empathic ability and had been unable to endure it.

His parents must have recognized the signs in their only son, as well, and that was why they rid themselves of him. How wicked of them to abandon him to his abusive uncle. How cruel to put him in a place where he'd be tortured by the emotions of so many people every day and night. How easily he might have followed in his grandfather's footsteps. More than once he had wished he could end it all.

He thought there was no more to be seen as the mirror lingered on the image of his grandfather's grave, but then it flickered and a series of scenes unfolded seeming to show contrasting scenarios involving the lieutenant: scenarios that included her, and those that did not. The lieutenant standing by Prince Zachary's side as he was crowned king, leading to a prosperous realm, juxtaposed to the lieutenant absent, and Zachary's brother, Prince Amilton, ascending to the throne and leading a realm gripped by chaos and dark forces, the roots and vines of Blackveil Forest taking hold across the country.

Wait, Tavin thought, *Amilton is supposed to ascend after Isen and Amigast, not Zachary.*

But his thought and the image of a castle in ruin were supplanted by other visions. The lieutenant talking to a girl with brown hair—he could not hear the words—who at first wore long blue skirts, but reappeared in another scene garbed in Rider green. She repelled an attack on Prince Zachary—*King* Zachary?—by foes that were blurred and moved too quickly in his vision to make out clearly. A quick sequence of scenes showed her engaged in heroic acts, sometimes Zachary beside her, or other Riders, but more often alone. Sometimes the enemies she faced were dark, very dark. One brutally tortured her. Interspersed among these swift images were moments in which the lieutenant appeared to be giving the girl support or advice. The girl clearly looked up to her. And what was that insignia on the lieutenant's shortcoat? *Colonel?* But there were no colonels in the messenger service.

In the alternate version without the lieutenant, the girl arrived at the castle after apparently having heard the call, but Amilton was king and the Riders in disarray. Some were executed as traitors, their heads planted on pikes before the castle gates alongside . . . Zachary's. Tavin lost track of the girl, but he could only guess she'd fallen to some ill fate, and as the vision pulled back to reveal a distant view of the castle, blackness swirled over the battlements. Figures flew aloft, swarmed across the clouds like impenetrable smoke. Winged, fanged, and clawed, they were terrible, demonic. He could not tear his gaze away as the creatures spread across the countryside. The shard forced him to watch the ravaging of villages, the ruination of the land. A cry stuck in his throat.

When at long last he was flung from that scene to another of ordinary smoke rising as if from a campfire, it was a feeling of great relief. He thought that would be the end of it, but the mirror jumped to a close image of a pouch of acorns being offered to a beautiful, golden lady who was surrounded by greenery and bore a rose blossom on her palm.

The mirror then simply shimmered to its normal silvery surface, and he found himself staring once more at his own warped reflection. He slammed the shard onto the table.

"What the hells was all *that?*" he demanded.

"Carefully, friend Tavin," the hermit said. He gingerly drew the shard to himself. "Take a moment to catch your breath."

Tavin's mind reeled, but he listened and allowed the golden glow coming down through the branches to caress him and once more fill his soul with peace. But it was a troubled peace.

"*What* was that?" he asked again, but this time quietly and in wonder.

"A little of the past, perhaps something clarifying," the hermit said.

"Yes, my grandfather. I'm not sure I wanted to know what I saw there."

"What you saw is that you are not the only one who has struggled with the empathic gift. It is not unusual for such a gift to run in families. Sadly, for your grandfather, there was no one to show him how to control it."

Tavin closed his eyes. If he had not been called, if he hadn't ridden north with the lieutenant, he would not have met the hermit and learned how to block out the emotions of others. Would his fate have been the same as his grandfather's had he not heard the call?

"The rest," the hermit said, "I believe are potential futures that rely on your lieutenant's presence or absence. Her absence, of course, being catastrophic."

"What could happen if I don't help her, you mean."

"Yes. This very moment we sit amidst great beauty, etherea in its most innocent and pure form, but there are forces at work that would poison it, that would destroy all that is good. You know what a fulcrum is?"

Tavin nodded. "Yes, a sort of support on which a lever balances or tilts."

"That is so. And your lieutenant is that fulcrum, or will be. She is the support for those who would tilt the lever to the side of light. Without her, others will be unable to save not only the realm of Sacoridia, but the world."

"*The world?*"

"Oh, yes," the hermit replied. "As surprising as it may

sound. But as much as she is the fulcrum, at this time now, you are the ground beneath her, the one who supports the fulcrum as sure and strong as solid bedrock. Or, you could be if you helped her." He paused, then leaned forward. "My friend Tavin, the fate of the world falls upon your shoulders."

THE SOLID GROUND UPON WHICH THE FULCRUM STANDS

Tavin's mouth dropped open. How could this be? He was a nobody from Adolind. A lowly messenger in training.

"There is something you should know about visions of the future," the hermit said. "The future is always in motion, always changing. The smallest thing can change its course. What you saw were possibilities of what *may* happen if the current line of events hold steady. Think of it as a boat on a river affected by waves and currents, landforms and weather. It may have to navigate hither and thither to reach its destination. The obstacles to navigation may in fact force a change in destination. Er, not that the future is a destination as it is always in motion, always moving forward, but you get the idea."

"All of this is dependent on me?" Tavin asked, still in disbelief.

"It *may* be," the hermit replied. "With the future, as I was saying, nothing is absolute. However, would you rather take a chance?"

In other words, if he did not help the lieutenant on the chance that everything would turn out fine despite his visions, he was playing against the odds, and losing meant that the world as he knew it would fall beneath some dark influence. If he did help the lieutenant, the odds for a better outcome increased.

"There is another aspect to this, albeit on a smaller scale," the hermit continued. "Your lieutenant is a human being who is suffering a great deal. You must decide whether it is humane to allow her suffering to continue."

"There isn't a lot I can do if she won't consent."

"You can keep trying," the hermit said. "Perhaps you will succeed in persuading her. It may not be the best tack, however, to accuse her of being unfit."

A wave of guilt washed over Tavin. No, he had only made the job harder for himself. He couldn't imagine how angry and defensive he'd made her, or how he would overcome it.

"Remember this golden light, the light of the wood. Bear it within, and perhaps that will aid you," the hermit said. "There is something else you should know. Even should you succeed, even if the world should hurtle on in a positive direction because of your actions, you should not expect thanks or acknowledgment of any kind. Few, if any, will understand the role you played, or that there was any danger to begin with."

That was normal, Tavin thought. He only got yelled at, accused of clumsiness, stupidity, any multitude of shortcomings. Why change things now? But he would do the thankless task. He would do it because the consequences of failing were too terrible to contemplate.

The hermit nodded as if hearing his thoughts. "Many of

the greatest deeds of this world are unknown, unsung— the names of heroes never known, never remembered."

Tavin sat in silent thought for a time processing all the hermit had told him and the ramifications of the visions he'd seen. Eventually he asked, "There were other images at the end. They seemed to be about something else. There was smoke, a handful of acorns. A golden lady with a rose in her hand."

The hermit adjusted his headdress, jostling a nuthatch perched on one of the tines of the antlers. It flapped its wings, regained its balance, and settled.

"Those scenes were unexpected," the hermit said. "I do not know what the smoke portends, and I assume the acorns have some symbolic reference to the oak. The lady? I know not."

"Maybe if we look again—"

"No, friend Tavin. One must not look too often into the future, for its constantly changing currents can unmoor one, leading to second-guessing and madness. Very few possess the strength of mind required to repeatedly observe the weft and warp of the universe that shapes our existence."

Tavin nodded. He didn't understand, precisely, about the fabric of the universe, but he hadn't really wanted to look into the shard again, anyway. The dark visions had been, well, dark, and clung to him like a shadow. Who wanted to see their future? Or, at least, too much of it? For all the hermit's words about a boat on a river and the flow of time, it was too easy to think of that future as predetermined. Madness lay in that, too.

One thing he was absolutely certain about was that he did not envy that brown-haired girl, that Green Rider of the future, whoever she was, if she was going to be critical to battling the great darkness.

"Before you leave," the hermit said, "I must warn you not to speak of what you've seen in the hollow of this ancient oak today. Speak nothing of the mirror, nor of the visions you witnessed. Though Abram is worthy, even he has not been invited within."

"Then why me?" Tavin asked.

"Because, my friend, you are the solid ground upon which the fulcrum stands."

That afternoon when Tavin returned to the waystation, the air had turned muggy hot and a few wisps of clouds drifted above, but not enough to suggest the rain the hermit had predicted.

The door and window of the cabin were wide open, but first he went to see the horses. Both were fine and nudged him for food.

"Not time yet, you silly nags."

He gave them both scritches and checked their water, which was at a good level and still clean. Then, taking a deep breath, he entered the cabin. The lieutenant was sitting up in bed and sharing a cup of tea with Abram.

"Ah, Rider," Abram said. "Welcome back. I trust you had a good visit with the hermit?"

Tavin nodded. He kept the golden light of the oak inside him, like a warm glowing ball that resided in his chest, and in his memory also, but he lowered a layer of his shielding to take a reading of the lieutenant's mood. She was, he found, calm and peaceful, but there were sharp edges around that peace.

"You have arrived at a good time," Abram said, "for I must resume scouting."

"It is not like I need a nursemaid," the lieutenant said.

Tavin raised his eyebrow, but Abram just smiled and replied, "And deny me the pleasure of your company? Being a queen's forester is lonely work, and it is a treat for me to have so fine a conversationalist with whom to spend the day."

The lieutenant's expression softened. "Well, in that case, visit anytime."

"Will do."

Tavin followed Abram outside and to the edge of the clearing. "What on Earth did you two talk about?"

"Many things," the forester replied. "Much about the royal court, the queen, the two young princes . . . and the future."

Abram's words, and his slight hesitation before "and the future," suggested to Tavin they had shared a concern about what a future with a King Amilton would mean for Sacoridia. If so, it was an interesting coincidence considering what Tavin had seen in the hermit's mirror. He'd never paid much attention to the affairs of his betters. His duty was to serve, but now his interest was definitely piqued.

"She ate some solid food and was awake for much of the time," Abram said. "She even got up and moved about for a bit, which is good. She should be getting back on her feet so she can regain her strength." He glanced back at the cabin. "She asked a fair bit about what you were up to visiting the

hermit and so forth, and all I knew to tell her was that you
were learning about your special ability."

"All right, thanks," Tavin said, and he wished Abram a
good day.

After Abram's departure, Tavin stared at the cabin and its
wide-open door with trepidation. He'd have to go in sooner
or later and be alone with her. He put one foot in front of the
other, not knowing how he'd convince her to let him help
her, but knowing he had to because Sacoridia's future de-
pended on it. Perhaps he could start with an apology.

She watched him as he entered.

"Need more tea?" he asked.

"No, thanks."

He checked the fire, then started going through one of
his saddlebags, searching for his sewing kit and a sock that
needed mending. When he found both and the wooden darning egg, he sat at the table and worked to thread a needle. He
was aware of her watching, which made his hands shake a
little, which in turn made it more difficult to thread the needle. When finally he succeeded, he began stitching.

"Someone taught you to sew," the lieutenant observed.

"Granny Olsted, a lady in my village," he said. "I'm not
very good." His cheeks burned, remembering the poor su-
turing job he had done on the lieutenant.

As if picking up on his thoughts, she said, "Stitching the
flesh of a bleeding person is a whole different order of sewing than repairing a hole in an old sock."

He gazed at the sock in one hand, and thread and needle in the other. It was a generous statement considering the

terrible scar she'd bear for the rest of her life thanks, at least in part, to him.

He eased out a breath and stabbed the sock with his needle. He might not be good at sewing, but he didn't dislike it. In fact, he found it calming. Focusing on it had allowed him to shut out the emotions of others, and now it gave him time to gather his courage for an apology.

"Not a common ability among young men, but a good one to have," she commented. "I might suggest to the captain we include it among the skills we teach new Riders during training."

He nodded, weaving the threads over the hole and steeled himself. "Um, Lieutenant, there's—"

"Tavin," she said at the same time.

They glanced at one another.

"I'll go first," she said. "There is something I have to say."

He was surprised to feel some discomfort from her, something akin to remorse.

"First, I would not be alive if not for you. From the little I recall, and from what Abram says you told him, your quick thinking and, yes, your sewing ability kept me from bleeding to death, and even as I was totally useless and wounded, you evaded the brigands and brought both of us safely to the waystation. Thank you."

"Any Rider would have—"

"Tavin," she said sharply, "that Rider was *you*. Take my words for what they are, an expression of gratitude. I am not sure just any Rider would have been so cool and quick thinking under those circumstances."

His cheeks warmed at the unexpected praise from the Ice Lady. He had not felt cool and quick thinking at the time. "I'm—I'm glad I could help" was all he could think to say.

"Second," she continued, "I owe you an apology. I treated you poorly and I am very sorry."

"You—?" He was incredulous. "No, I mean, I should be apologizing for—"

"For bringing me to my senses? Telling me I was not fit for duty? Well, that might have been pushing it a bit, but it got my attention. No, there is no need for you to apologize, though in any other situation you would have been crossing a line. But I crossed a line myself with my behavior when you were only trying to help."

"You've been wounded and fever sick," he began.

"True, but no excuses. I behaved poorly toward you and certainly not as a Green Rider or an officer ought. You did not deserve it. It's no wonder you left the waystation to spend time with the hermit when you could. I wouldn't have wanted to be around me, either."

Because her ability was what it was, he did not argue or deny that going to the hermit had been an escape. Instead, he replied, "He was very helpful about my ability."

A keen look ignited in her eyes that caused him a certain amount of unease at being the subject of her gaze. Once again he sensed the sharp edges around her otherwise calm demeanor.

"Tell me," she said, "how this hermit happens to know so much about Rider magic."

CONNECTION

The needle slipped and Tavin stabbed his thumb. "Ow!" He sucked on the wound and spat the blood into the fireplace where it hissed on the coals.

The lieutenant waited. Before Tavin spoke, there was a distant rumble of thunder.

"I don't know how the hermit knows magic," he said, and it was the truth. The lieutenant would discern as much with her ability. "He's been around a long time, so he knows a lot of stuff."

She peppered him with questions about the hermit—how long had he "been around," did he have a name, where was he from . . .?

"Imnatar," she mused after he told her what he knew. "I've not heard of these people."

"He says they're long gone, or merged with other peoples over time."

As the questions continued, he answered as well as he could whatever she asked. After all, the hermit hadn't said he couldn't. He was careful, however, to obey the hermit's wishes that he not mention the mirror shard or his visions of the future. He also said nothing about the hollow of the oak tree, but she hadn't seemed very interested in the tree anyway.

"I appreciate the mending the hermit did for me," she said when she ran out of questions, or rather when Tavin ran out of answers. "It's clear he is an unusual fellow. I've always felt there was more going on in the Green Cloak than appeared on the surface." She sat quietly as if deep in thought. She yawned a few times, her eyelids drooped, and she soon dozed off.

Tavin finished darning his sock while she slept. It was not neat work, but it would do. After he put his sewing kit away, he tended to chores: fed the horses, scrubbed dishes, and hauled in wood for their fire. The sky rumbled now and then while he worked, but a storm never materialized.

The lieutenant murmured in uneasy dreams. He considered intervening, but feared that if he did, it would cause her to resist him tenfold. In their conversation, even with her apologies, calm, and kindness, she was not far removed from the anger that burned just beneath the surface, her need to protect the wound that was all her ugly memories of what the Darrow Raiders had done.

He kept the cabin door open as he worked so he could keep an eye on her. He was sweeping the front step when she woke up and got out of bed. She stood there, balance wavering.

"Need help?" he asked.

"No." Her reply was fierce.

He chose not to interfere as she wobbled her way to the door. He moved aside so she could step over the threshold and follow the path to the outhouse. A couple times he almost threw his broom aside to run to her aid, but she made it under her own power, and she made it back, too. When she hauled herself onto the bed, she fell asleep almost immediately. It was not peaceful, and her distress leaked through his shields, but still he did not interfere.

The thunder had died off by the time she awakened a couple hours later. He offered her stew. The waystation was stocked with preserves and dried meat, so he had added some to the soup and thickened it with flour. She needed to start eating more solid food if she expected to regain her strength. She accepted the bowl and stared into it, stirring the contents.

"Flies in your stew?" he inquired.

"Hmm?" She glanced up at him.

"You were deep in thought."

"I guess I'm not quite awake. Tired."

"Your sleep was restless," he told her. "It can't help."

She gazed back down at her bowl. "I know."

"I could help you if you let me," he said quietly.

Her eyes blazed, and Tavin snapped his shields fully into place. He'd the sensation of both of them withdrawing miles apart from one another.

"I don't need your help," she said.

He snorted.

"What's that, Rider? You have something to say? Maybe that I'm unfit again?"

There was a harsh retort on the tip of his tongue. She might be his superior officer whom he was duty-bound to respect and obey, but he was also tired, tired of her mood swings and being snapped at. And shouldn't respect run both ways? Except, the words that were about to spill from his mouth were venomous and cruel, and far worse than calling her unfit. They would earn him no respect whatsoever, only the opposite.

He took a deep breath instead, and following the example set by Abram and the hermit, tried to radiate a sense of calm. It was hard not to just react, to say what came first upon his tongue, but then he remembered to release the negative energy into the ground. He felt an immediate easing, but he did not release it all. No, let her read that he wasn't a straw dummy for her to beat on.

He peeled away one layer of his shields, and then another, and as he did so, he realized that beneath her anger lay fear. Fear of revealing her true self, fear of letting her guard down, fear of the pain caused by her memories.

"I wish," he said, threading calm into his words, "that someone could have helped me a long time ago." Granny Olsted had been good to him, but she had not understood his empathic nature anymore than he had and could not help him in the way he needed. "The hermit calls this ability of mine a gift, but it's been nothing but a curse my whole life."

"You mean," she said, clearly in shock, her anger fading, "you had it *before* the call?"

He nodded. "My whole life, though the brooch makes it stronger. I didn't know what it was growing up, or that it was different from everyone else even though I got beat up for it and shunned. Working the common room of the Barefoot

Bride and not knowing how to block anyone out? Thought I was going mad. Closing myself in my little room was no help."

"Oh, Tavin. I'm sorry."

He was not finished. "I used to walk to a bridge that goes over a gorge just outside of town. I'd think about how jumping off it would solve my problems. My grandfather, it was always rumored, had killed himself. I've only just realized it's because he had the curse. Not easy when you can feel everyone's annoyance toward you, their hatred and disgust. Especially from my uncle. My parents shoved me off on him because they didn't know what to do with me, I guess. I assume my mother knew the signs from my grandfather. Maybe she thought it was just madness and didn't know how to cope. My uncle, he thought me simple and girly because I was so sensitive. Worthless. Constantly yelled at me to be a man."

The lieutenant shook her head and gazed again into her untouched bowl of stew. "I had no idea."

"As you can see, I didn't jump off the bridge because there were some who actually cared about me." Especially Granny Olsted. "And when I could get help finally from the hermit? I took it and haven't looked back. Still not easy keeping my shields up all the time. Tiring. Also, now that I think of it, like having your sight go dim, or food taste dull."

Silence fell between them. He sensed her remorse and pity. He didn't want her pity, but he kept it to himself, not wishing to destroy their tenuous connection.

Finally, she looked up and said, "I don't think there has been an empath among the Riders for a couple decades. My truth-telling ability, which is akin, hasn't been seen since Gwyer Warhein, about two hundred years ago."

"Do you suppose," he asked, trying not to insinuate he knew the answer, "there might be a reason why you, with your ability, were called after all this time?"

She laughed. "Like I have some destiny?"

"You did put down the Darrow Raiders. What if the brooches know when to call the Riders they need?"

That quieted her. "I don't know. It's an interesting thought, though. As for me, well, I'm just me. No one special. And, I expect the call to release me soon. It's overdue, actually."

If the visions he'd seen in the hermit's mirror were to be believed, she would stay a Rider for many more years. But he had to convince her to let him help her.

"Even so, it doesn't change the fact you are important to the Riders, the queen, and Prince Zachary. If you would let me help you, I would not be going into your head. I'd be lightening your load, making it easier for you to cope with the memories. And sleep. If you keep on the way you've been going, you won't heal. At least, not well."

"I don't know," she said.

Before he could reply, something small bounced off her head and splashed into her stew.

"Ow!"

He looked up and saw Winterberry perched on a rafter. The squirrel chirped.

The lieutenant picked an acorn out of her stew. "Good thing that wasn't hot anymore. What is it with the squirrels around here?"

Winterberry scurried along the length of the rafter, down the front of the chimney, and onto the mantel where she convulsed with hysterics.

Instead of expressing anger at the squirrel's presence in the cabin, the lieutenant sniffed the air. "Do you smell smoke?"

At first Tavin thought it was blowback from their cookfire, but then the back of his neck prickled with premonition. He peered through the window and spied an orange flicker through the woods.

He jumped to his feet. "Fire!"

FIRE

Without hesitation, Tavin grabbed one of his bedroll blankets off the floor and tore out through the door to the back of the cabin where he submerged the blanket into the spring and saturated it. As he sprinted back around the cabin, he saw the lieutenant standing in the doorway.

"If this gets bad, we may have to make a run for it," he told her.

He then charged across the clearing and through the wards toward the flames with his dripping mass of blanket. The wards, he thought, would not protect the station from fire. The flames were low to the ground thus far, not yet climbing the trees. A glance eastward showed that in the distance, the fire had progressed more and was, in fact, roaring to the tree-tops. The wind was calm, so that was in their favor.

He coughed at the smoke and kept throwing his blanket over the flames to smother them. All he could hope to do was stall the fire from burning its way toward the waystation.

To his consternation, a short time later, the lieutenant

joined him. She had dressed, put on boots, and girded herself with her sword. Just that should have been enough to exhaust her, but she carried another sopping wet blanket.

"You shouldn't be out here," he told her. "I don't want to have to carry you out."

"The horses are saddled just in case we have to run," she said, "and I don't trust this."

He eyed her saber again, wondering what it was she didn't trust. You couldn't fight fire with a sword. In any case, having the horses saddled would help. They would flee if the fire got too close to the waystation, or if it looked like it would flank them, but he was concerned she was drawing on reservoirs of energy she didn't have, which would make escape more difficult if he had to worry about her.

The woods were on the dry side, and the fire was liking the deadfall and brush. Having lived in heavily forested Adolind his whole life before the Rider call, he knew all too well how devastating a fire could be. He wondered if it had been a lightning strike that had caused it, but though it had thundered earlier, the lightning had been distant, not very active. Perhaps someone's campfire had gotten out of control.

The lieutenant withdrew and doubled over with hacking.

"Go back to the cabin," he told her.

"No."

Obstinate as always.

He kept working, his blanket singed and steaming. It seemed hopeless as he lost ground and the flames began to flare up tree trunks. His efforts did little to stem the progression of the fire.

"I think we should—" he began.

Just then, the rain the hermit had predicted began to fall. At first it was just a sprinkle, then it turned into a light but steady shower. Would it be enough to hinder the fire's progress?

"Tavin," the lieutenant said.

"Rain!" he shouted with a laugh.

"Tavin."

The sober tone of her voice caused him to look up. Men stepped out of the woods and surrounded them, and he staggered under the assault of their violent intentions despite his shields. So focused on firefighting had he been that he hadn't felt their approach. There were eight of them. The lieutenant unsteadily held her saber before her, shaking with fatigue. She could barely stand.

One of the men chuckled. "Told ya it would smoke 'em out of hiding, Ray. You owe me five silvers."

One of the others, presumably Ray, grumbled.

Tavin did not have his sword on him, just his longknife, which he drew.

"The Red Witch," a third man said. "Finally."

"It appears my reputation has preceded me," she said.

"I am surprised you're still alive," the man said, "after that injury you got. But not for much longer."

Sweat, or rain, slid down Tavin's face; he wasn't sure which. The fire hissed and crackled. Evil anticipation oozed from the men, so much so it made him ill.

"What do you say, boys," the man, clearly their leader, said. "Burn her alive? Isn't that what you do with witches?"

The men laughed.

"You will have to catch me first," the lieutenant said. There was much strength in her voice, but Tavin felt her undercurrent of weakness and fear.

"Fine," the man said. "Should be easy."

The man thought it a great joke, Tavin knew. He was eager to play with his prey as a cat with a mouse. Tavin was aware of the men also keeping a close watch on him for any move he might make, but they were most interested in the lieutenant.

With a smug look on his face, the man drew his sword and half-heartedly batted at the lieutenant's. She responded with a fierce round of blows. Tavin felt the man's surprise, but he also felt what it cost the lieutenant.

The man parried her thrusts as his companions laughed and cheered him on. The lieutenant even sliced through his sleeve, though apparently not enough to make him bleed. Tavin sensed his embarrassment, which made him angry and dangerous.

He struck viciously at the lieutenant. Miraculously she pushed it off, but when he swept his sword back, it sent her saber flying and she collapsed to her knees. The man leaped over to grab her by the hair and held the blade to her throat. Tavin made to leap to her defense but the other men grabbed him. They pulled his knife out of his hand and wrenched his arm behind his back. The fire spat and steamed as the rain came down more heavily. Thunder rolled.

"Look at me," said the leader. He yanked the lieutenant's hair. "I got the witch who defeated the Darrow Raiders. We'll burn her, but not the head. We'll need that."

Tavin felt the leader's elation, which arose from an insatiable need for acclaim. Taking down the Red Witch would fulfill that need, at least for a while, and put him in a place of strength over the ragtag gangs tussling for power in the absence of the Darrow Raiders. Tavin sensed the man's cunning and charisma that drew others to follow him. He craved their unwavering adulation, and he'd do anything to secure it. Cruelty for him was a means to an end that he exercised without remorse or mercy. He would demonstrate to his men in his handling of the Red Witch that he was an even stronger leader than Urz had been.

The words of the hermit came back to Tavin: *My friend, you have an empathic ability that can help others like your lieutenant, but with your level of power, it is also a weapon.*

Tavin had used it as a weapon and killed a man. Could he take on eight enemies at once?

He could feel how each man, individually and as a group, seethed with dark anticipation. They'd captured highly desirable prey. They were not strangers to committing violence. They were thieves and murderers all, and like their leader, spared no mercy for even the most innocent of victims.

Tavin breathed deeply of the smoke-laden air. Beneath the acrid stench of burning was the scent of forest freshened by rain, the earthiness of moss and loam, the resilience of green leaf and stem. He girded himself with it, wrapped the spirit of the wood about himself like armor, then loosened his shields and absorbed all the emotions and memories of cruelty borne by the men.

With an exhalation, he turned memory and emotion into a weapon and delivered unto them the full measure of their crimes so that they experienced their own violence from the point of view of their victims. His power coursed and crackled through every fiber of his being as he forced them to know fear, pain, and, worst of all, grief. He fed it to them unrelentingly. They cried and threw their arms over their faces as if to ward off some brutality, in the process releasing Tavin. The leader's sword slipped from his hand and he let go the lieutenant's hair.

"Make it stop!" they cried. They begged for their mommas and called upon the gods for mercy. The fire glittered on their rain- and tear-soaked faces. Tavin did not stop but grounded all their negative energy back into them, all their cruelty and evil, rendering them harmless and pathetic as they crawled on their bellies or rolled on the ground wailing. One of the men threw himself into the fire in order to make the torment stop.

The lieutenant was but a blur in Tavin's vision. She was yelling, but he could not hear. His awareness was only for the outpouring of power he continued to unleash on the men, of all the hurts he himself had experienced throughout his life, of all his wrath that had never before had such an outlet. He laughed in euphoria with the realization that he possessed power enough to reach and destroy his uncle, his parents, all

the girls who had ridiculed him, all the boys who had beat
and humiliated him, and, yes, the whole of the lands if he so
chose. Such power was his!

"Tavin!" the lieutenant cried. "Stop! Enough."

"No, I—"

She shook him. *"Tavin!"*

He raised his arm to strike her, to ground his rage into
her for all her arrogance, for all she'd put him through, for
all her anger and annoyance with him.

Peace, friend Tavin, came the hermit's calming voice into
his mind. *Be easy. You have punished those who needed pun-
ishing. Be easy and rest now.*

Tavin stopped. Let it go, all the anguish he had inflicted.
He was no monster. He did not wish to possess that kind of
power. It continued without him, took on a life of its own
that consumed the men from the inside out. He sealed off his
shields, the silence bringing to him such serenity, such relief.
He gazed at the lieutenant to see how she fared even as the
skies opened and a torrent of rain fell. She stood nearby watching him closely. He was lightheaded after the exertion of using
his ability. Spent. He collapsed.

Man-shaped flames danced before him with howls of agony. Awake, or had he descended into the five hells? The lieutenant appeared, saber shining in the flame. She was soaked
through, but her expression was fierce, the personification,
he thought, of Valora, goddess of war, of vengeance, of joy.
She slid her blade home into the man of flame. He gave a final howl and fell.

Tavin sank into darkness once more.

———

"Tavin. Tavin?"

He looked up, saw her hazel eyes, and rain dripping off her hair. She patted his cheek.

"Tavin!"

No, he thought. Too tired. He felt himself lifted off the ground and hefted over a strong shoulder. He fell into nothingness again.

A SENSE OF WELL-BEING

Tavin awoke warm and dry beneath the covers of the bed to the sound of rain pattering on the roof. Winterberry sat on the windowsill, scaling a spruce cone. All about was the stench of wet smoke. In the gray daylight, he saw the lieutenant there, sitting at his bedside in a chair, asleep. Her oversized Rider shirt was splashed with dirt and blood. It looked as if her wound had reopened and bled some. Her features were placid, and her red hair glinted with gold even in the dull light. If he ignored the wounding on her chin and neck, she looked an untroubled young woman, innocent, one who would be the light of one's village and courting—vibrant and comely. Not the Green Rider who ruthlessly brought the Darrow Raiders to heel or had driven a sword into a burning man like an avenging goddess. What would her future bring?

Her long eyelashes fluttered open and she shifted in her chair. She started when she realized Tavin was awake.

She sat up straight. "Tavin? How do you feel?"

"Hungry," he admitted, "and like I'm not the one who is supposed to be in this bed."

"The hermit said you should stay abed for a while after you woke up."

"He was here?"

"Briefly to check on you, and to fix me up." She grimaced, and he knew he'd guessed right about her reopening her wound.

He was glad to learn, however, the hermit was all right after the fire.

"He wants you to go see him when you can," she said, slowly rising to step up to the hearth. "Odd fellow."

Tavin couldn't argue there.

She brought him a bowl of stew.

He looked at it, then at her. "This is a bit of a reversal."

She smiled. "Don't get used to it."

While he ate, she told him what had happened while he was unconscious, that the men who had lured them out by setting the fire and then attacked them had gone mad. She hadn't understood their behavior until the hermit explained it to her.

"I knew you were doing something to them, but at the time I didn't know exactly what. You turned their own minds against them," she said. "All the horrible things they did in their lives they were made to experience as the victims. Over and over again."

She told him how they bashed their heads against rocks to make it stop, pleaded and cried for the torment to end. She had stabbed the fellow who had caught fire to prevent him from spreading flames through the woods, but the others she left to suffer.

"They were all dead by this morning," she said. "They got what they deserved. While you were with the hermit, Abram told me about the gangs he's been scouting and chasing out of the queen's wood. They were looking for us. Me. So I had my suspicions about how the fire started, and it seems I was right. It was the sort of thing Urz would have done."

Thoughts of the power he had unleashed made Tavin shudder. He had almost loosed it on the whole of the realm. He looked at his hands, expecting them to be the claws of an evil monster. How had he come by such power? Might he be tempted to use it one day for ill?

Before he could dwell on it, the lieutenant continued with her story. Abram, she said, had arrived in the midst of it all with a crew of foresters to cut a line through the woods to break the progress of the fire. The rain had enabled them to take the upper hand over the conflagration before it caused much damage. The crew continued to keep an eye on the area. Despite the usual competition between foresters, there was a spirit of cooperation when it came to fires. After all, fire did not discriminate, and a disaster for one could mean disaster for all.

"It's Abram who brought you into the cabin," the lieutenant said, "but I'm sure you guessed that much."

He had.

Winterberry chirped on the windowsill.

"That squirrel has been sitting there all day," she said.

"She's a friend."

Winterberry watched them for a moment, then chucked

what was left of her spruce cone into the cabin. That accomplished, she scurried off into the wild. The lieutenant raised a single copper eyebrow.

They sat in silence for a time. Tavin kept his shields loose, but sensed no troubling emotions from the lieutenant. Minutes passed, each submerged in their own thoughts.

Then, without warning, the lieutenant said, "Yes."

"What?" Tavin said, feeling as if he'd missed some vital part of a conversation. "Yes what?"

"Yes, I will accept your help."

He nearly jumped out of bed he was so pleased to hear those words, but he feared any outward expression of elation would scare her off. Instead, he stilled himself and replied, "It would be my honor."

It was not until the next day that Tavin felt up to invoking his ability again, and the lieutenant needed rest herself after all the activity the night of the fire. He'd gladly given the bed up for her, and she was so exhausted she slept undisturbed by nightmares.

When she was ready, they went outside. She spread a blanket by the paddock for them to sit on. The scent of smoke lingered in the air and the near woods were scarred by the fire, but it wasn't nearly as bad as he had feared. What had become of the bodies of the men who had attacked them he knew not, nor did he care.

The horses watched them with interest from the paddock

fence. Winterberry sat on a mossy rock and nibbled on a mushroom.

"What do we do?" the lieutenant asked.

"I open my shields so I can read your emotions." He chose his words carefully, not wishing to give her cause to change her mind. "Right now I can feel that you are both nervous and determined." Before she could react, he added, "I am not in your head to know that. Your emotions sort of flow off you, and I, er, receive them. It's the same with everyone and just the result of my dropping my shields."

He then explained how he could accept her emotional energy and ground it. "It's like I said before, just lifting the weight off your shoulders so it's easier to cope. I won't go into your head or your dreams unless you request it."

"All right." She rested her hands on her thighs. "What's next?"

This was the hard part. This was where she was apt to change her mind and walk away, and there was no making it easier on her.

"Tell me," he said, "about Sam."

He felt how his words thrust into her like a dagger of grief, but there was also an eagerness there, an eagerness to speak of the man she had loved so much. She did not walk away. She did not hold back.

"We met at the Day of Aeryon races," she said. "His mates had gotten him drunk the night before, got him to make a bet that he subsequently lost, which in turn required him to enter one of his mules in the three-quarter race." She chuckled, seemed far away with the memory.

Sam, she told him, had been up against a friend of hers on a fast messenger horse, so they'd exchanged some words. She mocked his mule. He made an impertinent remark about her red hair. She did not bet on him, and he did not come close to winning, but damn if she hadn't been entirely charmed as he came loping down the final stretch far behind everyone else, waving his hat to the spectators as though he were a prince in a royal parade. No one remembered who had won the race that day, but everyone remembered Sam and his mule.

As she spoke of Sam, Tavin grounded her emotional energy. At times it was light when she remembered something humorous, and less so when the grief threatened to swamp her.

What he hadn't told her was that he was projecting calm and peace to her so she could actually continue sharing her memories. When she spoke of the Darrow Raiders and what they had done to her fellow Riders and Sam—not in detail, but enough that Tavin could imagine—was when he worked hardest to ground the negative energies and grief, and send her calm.

The emotional wounds were deep, stuck into her like tentacles. He then remembered the golden light of the great oak he'd stored within himself and slowly fed it to her. The tentacles gradually lost hold, and the imprints they left behind filled with the golden light.

When it was done, they were both a little breathless. All he felt from the lieutenant before he pulled up his shields once more was a sense of well-being.

They were both exhausted, and before Tavin lost consciousness, he told her, "I did not remove any of your actual emotions, just the energy. The grief remains, as do the happy memories. We can do this again if you wish."

As consciousness faded away, he thought, but could not swear to it, that she kissed his cheek with a featherlight touch and covered him with her side of the blanket.

SPIRIT OF THE WOOD

By the next day, the lieutenant was almost a different person. Her features were softer; she did not snap at him. Little of the Ice Lady he had known remained. She chatted congenially about soup and horse manure. Her physical wounds were still mending, so she had to rest a lot, and she was by no means ready for riding, but she could take care of herself so that finally he could go visit the hermit.

Feeling the spirit of the wood came effortlessly now, but when he stepped into the glade of the great oak, he found devastation. The greenery around the oak was charred. It appeared the fire had destroyed a swath of forest in the area and killed the oak. The limbs of the huge tree had crashed to the ground and still smoldered. What remained of the trunk was a blackened stump. No birds sang; no squirrels chased one another around the remains. No life seemed to stir at all.

"No," Tavin whispered.

"Ah, friend Tavin," the hermit called, sounding as cheerful as ever as he emerged from the woods. "I was wondering when you might find your way here."

"The oak . . ." Tavin could barely find his voice.

"Yes, my friend, the mighty one has fallen. The creatures who called it home fled as they could. Others were not so lucky." He gestured to a tiny cairn on the glade's edge where there was still green vegetation. "Poor Raincloud. He was too old and arthritic to run, and the smoke overcame him."

"I'm so sorry." Unexpected grief caught in Tavin's throat. Grief for a fat, old squirrel.

"It would have been better had he passed peacefully in his sleep," the hermit replied, "but he had a good long life, longer than most of his kind. Now come, tell me how you and the lieutenant fare."

Tavin followed him to uncharred ground, and they sat where there was a ring of boulders crusty with lichens. He told the hermit about the events of the night of the fire, about how he used his ability to destroy the eight men who had set the fire and come for the lieutenant.

"I felt . . . powerful," he said falteringly. "Too powerful, like I could take down the whole of the realm, and I wanted to. I wanted to destroy it all, and that power was within me."

The hermit nodded and softly said, "Yes, it *is* within you."

Tavin shuddered. "I'm a monster."

"No, my friend. Your good sense and your good heart prevailed. You rejected inflicting destruction beyond the bad men."

"Only because the lieutenant was there and . . ." He scratched his head. "I heard your voice."

"You did not use that power," the hermit reiterated. "You did not go down that path, and you now recognize your strength."

"Am I not a danger to all?"

"You are wise to it now. And what did you do once the need to shatter all calmed?"

Tavin laughed. "I fainted."

"And when you recovered?"

"After I recovered, the lieutenant finally agreed to accept help." He described how he'd gone about working through the emotions with which she'd been burdened.

"You see?" the hermit said. "It is not in your nature to destroy, but to mend."

"I gave those men a terrible death."

"They were a danger to you, and you were defending yourself and your lieutenant. Remember what the mirror showed and what the future might be like had she not survived. Sometimes, as gentle and kind as we try to be, even as we celebrate the spirit of the wood and the life within, there is a time that one must go to battle for a greater good." A tiny green caterpillar crawled along the hermit's sleeve. "The pupil has exceeded the master, and now we have true hope for that greater good, hope for the future."

Tavin leaned in as if to confide a secret, though no one else was around to hear. "Were those visions really real? Those futures?"

"Real enough, my friend. But now that you have helped the lieutenant, the outlook is more positive. Of course there are a thousand things significant and insignificant that can change the course of the future, but at present we are on a good track."

"Good. I would not have guessed the lieutenant to be so important in all this."

"She will not recognize it in herself." The hermit found a leaf for the caterpillar to crawl onto, and placed it on the ground. "You did not realize your own significance, and you will be there for her while she continues to heal. A time will come, however, when she is the fledgling on the edge of the nest ready to fly. Her wounds will have mended enough and may indeed be her strength."

"I saw the smoke in the mirror," Tavin said, "but did not know what it meant."

"Such is the way of looking into the future. It is often too cryptic and the warning is missed."

"What will you do now?" Tavin gestured to the ruins of the oak.

"The fire destroyed my cabin," the hermit replied, "but I have gathered together what has survived and I am going to wander. Yes, inspired by that book of yours, I am going to go see what the world looks like these days."

"But—but . . ." Tavin's lower lip quivered at the idea of the hermit going away. "What about the spirit of the wood? The squirrels and the bees?"

The hermit hopped off his rock. "The bees and squirrels will go on as they always have. They've no need for one crazy, old hermit. After all, the spirit of the wood is not going anywhere. Come see."

Tavin followed him to the burned, hollow stump of the once great oak.

"Look within, my friend, and you will see the spirit is

vibrant as ever, but first, a gift." He passed Tavin a pouch full of acorns. "They are from this giant, ancient tree, the next step in the cycle of life, eh? Some are for you. Plant them well. They will remain viable until you are ready to plant them. Think of me as they sprout and grow. The rest are for . . . well, I am not sure, but you will know to whom to give them, and when." He clapped Tavin's shoulder. "We will be friends always, even when many miles divide us. Now seek the spirit of the wood in the hollow. I have left some things there for you. And remember, the spirit is within you, too."

Tavin smiled and carefully tied the pouch of acorns to his belt. Then he stepped through what was once a mere crack, but now was a gap widened by burning. Charred debris littered the ground, but amid the devastation in the very middle, the tiniest sprout of an oak poked up from the ashes, a single emerald leaf aglow in dazzling gold light. The great oak would continue in its progeny, and as the hermit had said, the spirit of the wood remained.

Nearby, on a piece of clear ground were two jars, one of honey, the other of healing paste. The lieutenant's physical wounds would continue to benefit from the hermit's mending expertise. The jars sat upon an oblong object carefully wrapped in oilskin. He knew what it was without opening it. The hermit had attached a note.

Remember, young Tavin, to have empathy for others is a strength, not a curse, not a weakness. You have changed the future. I know you will use your gift wisely and well. I will wander off into the

*world—travel opens the mind and the heart, does it
not? You have done so for me, my friend.*

"You don't have to give the book back," Tavin said over
his shoulder.

No one answered. He carried his gifts outside the burned
hollow.

"Hermit?"

He walked all around, even found the burned remains of
the cabin, but no sign of the hermit. His grief was immense
for the hermit was the only one who had truly understood
him and his affliction, and had been able to help him. As he sat
on one of the rocks where they had conversed earlier, mourn-
ing the departure of his friend, Winterberry scolded him.

"I am being ridiculous, aren't I," he told her. "It's not as
if he's died. He has simply reawakened his interest in the world
and gone traveling. This is a good thing, and I should rejoice
instead of mourn. How lucky for those who will meet him
along the way, just as I was lucky to be his friend and learn
from him."

The hermit, he reflected, had saved him, saved him from
the torment of his ability, possibly even saved his life. That,
in turn, had allowed him to help the lieutenant, who, it was
hoped, would help a brown-haired girl who was somehow
important to the future of the realm and the world.

He pressed his book to his chest. His heart still hurt, but as
long as he held the spirit of the wood inside, the hermit would
always be close by.

A couple weeks later, Abram escorted Tavin and the lieutenant through the woods. After all the events that had made their stay at the waystation so fraught, the lieutenant had finally given the message from the queen to Abram, and he in turn gave them a response to present to the queen. Something about lumber for new ships.

Over the passage of two weeks, the lieutenant had recuperated to a point where she no longer tired so easily and could ride. They spent the time reading. He read to her from *Ona-Holean-Lo: My Travels Through the Cloud Islands,* and like the hermit, it reignited his desire to see new places. He supposed he would as a Green Rider.

They also passed the time playing cards, games which she usually won, and he continued to help her when she wished it. He helped banish the nightmares that plagued her, and listened if she needed to talk. He thought that the cracked mirror of her dreams must no longer be quite so fractured. He also concluded that now some of her emotional wounds were mending, she would connect more easily with her Riders and be a better leader for it.

"Here we are," Abram said. The woods parted, revealing the North Road. He'd no problem keeping up with them though they were mounted and he was on foot. "Do not push yourself, Laren. You do not want to undo all the healing."

"We'll go slow," she replied.

"I'll make sure of it," Tavin said. Winterberry, perched on his shoulder, chirped her agreement.

"It was good to see you despite the circumstances," the forester told the lieutenant, "and good to meet you, Rider Tavin Bankside."

They shook hands.

"If you should need work after you are done with the Green Riders," Abram added, "you'd make a fine forester. I can put in a good word with the queen if you are interested. Not every man would seek to put out a forest fire. Most would run."

"The man who runs is probably the smart one," the lieutenant said with a wry lilt to her voice.

They laughed and then said their final goodbyes. Abram Rust lumbered back into the woods, leaving only a trail of pipe smoke behind him.

Tavin held his arm out to a low-hanging branch. "It's your turn," he told Winterberry.

The squirrel protested.

"Come now, we've had this discussion. You won't be happy in the city and this is your home. Someone, after all, needs to keep an eye on the baby oak."

Winterberry sighed, then sprang from his arm onto the branch. She harangued them until they rode out of earshot.

"Squirrels," the lieutenant said.

"Squirrels," he agreed.

He'd be back to check on Winterberry and the new oak, he was sure of it, though no magical visions had told him so. Some things you just knew. In the meantime, he'd carry the golden glow of the spirit of the wood within him, no matter where he went.

"Lieutenant," he said, "what do you say we have a little race when we reach North?"

"We shouldn't gallop through town," she replied. "It wouldn't be seemly."

"Not a galloping race. I'm thinking a slow race. The slowest of us wins."

"A slow race," she murmured. "I wonder what the towns-folk will make of that?" She laughed. "Well, I can't resist a good wager."

"Excellent." He clapped Goose's neck. He was happy to be on the road again, and, at least for the moment, the future was on track.

EPILOGUE

Seventeen years later . . .

Laren Mapstone, captain of His Majesty's Messenger Service, watched from Rider stables as F'ryan Coblebay rode away at a slow trot on his chestnut gelding, Condor. He was heading off on a dangerous mission to Mirwell Province to contact one of the king's spies within Lord-Governor Mirwell's court. He was to retrieve any intelligence the spy, another Green Rider by the name of Beryl Spencer, might have to report. Thanks to Beryl and the Riders who collected her intelligence, several assassination attempts on Zachary's life had been thwarted.

Lord Mirwell, never a supporter of Zachary's, was providing refuge to Zachary's exiled older brother, Amilton, who had been crown prince until King Amigast thought better of it and named Zachary his successor to the throne instead. Supplanted as heir and high king, Amilton seethed with anger and hatred, and was the perfect pawn for Mirwell to mold for his own interests. A very tricky situation for F'ryan to navigate safely as Mirwell's suspicions about spies grew, and possibly an incendiary one should he be intercepted. He was, however, the right Rider for the job.

She did not doubt that somewhere along the path that crossed castle grounds, a certain young noble lady also watched his departure.

She turned to head back to officers quarters when someone called out to her.

"Captain! Captain Mapstone!"

She halted and gasped, startled to see a man—a post rider—with a string of pack mules jogging her way. One of the mules was white. She felt lightheaded and wavered for a moment.

Sam, she thought and briefly closed her eyes.

By the time the post rider reached her, she had regained her equilibrium. Every time she encountered one, however, no matter how many years ago Sam had been murdered, she still felt a mix of hope, grief, and shock all balled into a mere moment of turmoil that was like a punch to her heart.

"Captain," the fellow said, catching his breath, "I've got a package for you from that big forester up by North."

"Abram Rust?" she said in surprise. She had not seen or heard from him in years.

"Aye, ma'am. Let me get it out for you."

Another wave of vertigo crested upon her as he started unbuckling one of the packs on his white mule. A flash of a nightmare vision. She forced it from her mind when the post rider pulled out a square package wrapped in canvas and tied with twine. It was about the size of a loaf of bread.

"Here ya go," he said cheerfully, and placed it in her hands. "Have a good day now."

He clucked his mules away, and she mumbled a farewell. She carried the package, which had some substance to it but wasn't too heavy, to her quarters. Inside, she cleared off a messy section of the table that served as her desk and set the package on it.

Tucked beneath the twine was a folded letter with a plain red wax seal. When she opened it, she found Abram's neat penmanship.

Greetings, Laren,

I send you the difficult tidings that our friend Tavin Bankside has passed the shores of this Earthly domain and resides now with the gods to walk among the stars. He had been ill for some time with a cancerous growth the menders could not heal. In the end, he was comfortable and peaceful. We have put him to rest in the glade where the great oak once grew, in the shade of the new oak. I think he'd be pleased. Sadly, though we gave Goose much attention afterward, and intended to bring him to Sacor City to live out his years among other messenger horses as Tavin wished, he would not leave his master's graveside and followed him in death two days later after a bout of colic that could not be resolved. He was put to rest in the glade beside his Green Rider.

Tavin requested that I send you this box he made and its contents upon his passing.

The rest consisted of condolences and Abram's personal sorrow at the passing of a friend, and apologies that he could not bring the news in person.

Laren leaned back in her chair stunned. The call had released Tavin within a year after their training foray to the waystation near North. She'd heard nothing of his ill health, had not heard anything of him in a very long time.

A knock came on her door and she was startled from her reverie. "Come."

Her lieutenant, Patrici Brandt, poked her head in. "Captain? I have those reports you requested."

"Ah. Thank you."

Patrici brought in a bundle of papers and set them on the edge of the table. "Something wrong, Captain?"

Laren's shock at Abram's news about Tavin must have shown on her face. "I've just learned that a former Rider, a friend, has passed."

Patrici stilled. "Who?"

"His name was Tavin Bankside. Before your time as a Rider. He was with me when this happened." Laren touched the scar on her neck. It had healed, but in a discolored form, making it stand out against her skin even more than it would have otherwise. She did not blame Tavin's haphazard sutures for causing the discoloration. The castle menders had said scars just healed that way sometimes.

Patrici's eyes widened and her lips rounded into an *oh*. "He was the empath, wasn't he?"

"Yes," Laren replied, "and he used his gift to help me."

She had learned to trust her lieutenants with personal information that she couldn't share with other subordinates. As the leader of the Green Riders, she needed to maintain a certain amount of distance from them. Too much familiarity eroded good order and discipline. Still, she needed someone to confide in, and it was Tavin who had advised her when she made captain to trust in the discretion of her lieutenant, so she did. This way she did not have to hold so much in and bear the burden of it solely on her own shoulders.

"He wasn't a Rider long," she told Patrici. "And when his brooch abandoned him, he traveled for a time, then accepted a position as a royal forester somewhere in the Green Cloak. He liked being alone. It was easier on him being away from people because of his gift."

"He was still empathically sensitive after his brooch abandoned him?" Patrici asked.

Laren nodded. "He had been before he heard the call, too, which made for a difficult childhood."

Patrici gave a low whistle. "I can believe it."

"His gift was a torment to him. Fortunately, he had learned to protect himself from the emotions of others, but just having to shield himself all the time was exhausting. The forestry position was perfect for him." She described how he had died, and the passing of Goose, too.

"I'm so sorry, Captain," Patrici said. "Perhaps we can honor him in some way."

"Yes, that would be good." She'd light a candle for him in the chapel of the moon, and she would speak of him at the next all-Rider meeting. She would also add his name to the list of the Riders she had known who were gone. These she kept in a file that would one day be handed over to the next captain. So much of Rider history was lost or otherwise unknown that she was determined to keep detailed records of her time in the messenger service so perhaps one day they would help some Green Rider captain of the future.

The bell down in the city rang out and Patrici looked up. "I'm sorry, Captain, but I am due to meet with the stable master. If you need to talk later, let me know."

"Thank you, Patrici."

When her lieutenant left, Laren sat in the dim light of her quarters and contemplated the package. Memories of her and Tavin's time at the North waystation came afresh to her. She could not remember it all, of course, because she'd been sick, fevered, out of her head. The physical wound had torn off the scab that had thickened over the emotional wound of Sam's death, and those of her friends, at the hands of the Darrow Raiders. Her memory of the hermit was particularly clouded, what he looked like, sounded like. She recalled asking Tavin about him but remembered only that he said he had come from a people called the Imnatar. Regardless, she was grateful for him using his mending skills to halt the festering of her wound. There was no question she would have died otherwise.

Then there was Tavin himself, kindly and patiently trying to help her despite her temper. She'd been hot-headed, angry, and had lashed out. Eventually he'd brought her around and was able to help her cope with her consuming grief. Thanks to him, she started to live again, and even smile now and

then. She did not know what might have become of her had
she not accepted his help. It was a dark path she did not wish
to contemplate too closely.

At last she summoned the courage to open the package.
She hoped it did not contain a squirrel. Even in her sadness,
she chuckled at the thought.

She cut the twine, and the canvas and inner padding fell
away to reveal a beautiful, unstained box of light oak. It still
smelled of fresh-sawed wood. On the lid, the winged horse
symbol of the Green Riders, and the evergreen symbol of the
royal foresters, had been carved.

Inside she found a pouch full of acorns, an old book
about travel in the Cloud Islands that she recalled he had
cherished, and a silver coin. Tucked into the oilskin wrapped
around the book was a note from Tavin.

Dear Colonel Mapstone,

She halted right there and laughed. A joke from Tavin?
He knew full well that the highest ranking officer in the
Green Riders was captain. She started over.

Dear Colonel Mapstone,
    My days grow short, I think. The menders dose
me for the pain so that I may remain comfortable,
though I've asked them to withhold it for a little
while so I can be clear-headed to write you. I have
asked Abram to send you the items in this box once
I am gone, and Goose, too, who is getting on in years,

*but is sound. He will do best, I think, surrounded
by other Green Rider horses. Please take some
time to give him scratches behind his ears and the
occasional treat. He has always been my best friend.*

She paused reading, a great lump forming in her throat.

*I hope you will find a place on your shelf for the
book. I read to you from it while you were
recuperating in the waystation. Remember? It was
given to me by the one person who was truly kind
to me when I was a boy. Thanks to this book, I was
inspired to travel the lands, as well as the Cloud
Islands after my tenure with the Green Riders
ended. I saw much that was amazing and beautiful,
and met many interesting people. It has been a full
life, and my years of wandering among my happiest.
As a result, I do not fear what lies ahead, or regret
that my time is ending.*

*As for the coin, well, all these years I never paid
my lost wager for our "slow" race through North.
You and Bluebird made an art of slow walking, and
I do not think the citizens of that town will ever
forget it.*

Here she laughed through her tears.

*As a royal forester, I lived in wonder at the natural
world around me. The Green Cloak is truly*

magical, and I embraced the spirit of the wood.
Goose, Winterberry (and her descendants), and I
explored and patrolled the forest's extent. After the
fire near the waystation all those years ago, the
hermit had given me many acorns from the great
oak that had survived the flames. Some I planted in
places long forgotten or unknown by others around
the Green Cloak, and visited them as they grew
from mere sprouts into sure and strong saplings.
The spirit of the wood is ever strong, and these
young oaks will ensure it remains so.

I am giving you the stewardship of the rest of the
acorns. They will stay viable until the time comes
for them to be planted, but Colonel, only one is for
you, so do plant it with care. The rest (and this will
sound strange) are for the golden lady of the rose.
Alas, I will not be here to give them to her, so I
entrust you with this duty in my stead. You will one
day recognize who she is and when it is time to pass
them on to her. She will know what to do with
them. I can say no more than that.

Well, that was rather cryptic, Laren thought. But there
was more.

I was not supposed to mention the golden lady,
but too late now, eh?
There is something else I am not supposed to
mention, but I can't help myself because I feel it is

*too important. There is a brown-haired girl. She
will appear a commoner who will hear the call. She
is significant to the future of the realm, and she will
need your help and leadership. You will be her role
model. Do not let her down.*

Doubly cryptic. A brown-haired girl? There were so many
in the world, even among the Green Riders. How would she
even know who he meant? Did he mean her adopted daugh-
ter, Melry? Well, she'd just try to be a good role model for all
her Riders and any other young people who came into her
life. But how did Tavin even know these things? Had he developed some precognitive ability? Sadly it was too late to
find out.

*Finally, I wish to remind you that you've many
friends who love you. I am one of them. You are
strong and courageous, but in difficult times your
friends will see you through. Alas, I am unable to
remain among them.*

*Be happy and in peace, Laren Mapstone, and I
hope you will remember well of me.*

*Yours,
T. Bankside*

Laren sagged in her chair awash in a range of emotions,
half-laughing through tears, wishing Tavin were there to help
her with her emotions even as she grieved for him. In peace,

indeed. Without him that peace would have been elusive. Her one solace was that he said he'd led a happy and fulfilling life after his time as a Green Rider. How many people could say the same in the end? She rubbed her tears away. She'd never gotten to see the great oak, wasn't really sure where it was in relation to the waystation. Perhaps next time she was up north Abram could show her so she could properly pay her respects at Tavin's grave. Would the spirit of the wood allow her to enter the glade of the oak?

She rolled one of the acorns around on her palm. It was a gift of life for the future. The trees would grow and become home for many kinds of wildlife, provide forage for some creatures, and refuge for others. Their leafy canopies would create shade on summer days and bright beauty in autumn. All out of a tiny acorn like a miracle. It was the magic that was the spirit of the wood, no matter the troubles of the world.

Thank you, Tavin, she thought, *for the gift that was you, and this reminder that life carries on and flourishes.*

ACKNOWLEDGMENTS & STUFF

The book you hold in your hands was twenty-five years in the making. *What? This novella? I know you write slowly, but . . .* Ahem, not exactly what I meant. I mean, my first book, *Green Rider,* was published in 1998, so this is a celebration of that feat. Everything that has come after has built upon the creation and release of that book, including this novella. 1998 feels like ancient times these days, and much has changed since then. I daresay I no longer hand in a manuscript via snailmail, and I'm not quite as young as I once was. (My characters have aged much more slowly. Frankly, I'm jealous.) I won't go into the whole origin story of *Green Rider* and my writing career as it is documented elsewhere (see *The Dream Gatherer*, my previous novella and collection of Green Rider stories. The book, which celebrates an earlier anniversary, includes the story of how *Green Rider* came to exist.)

I will say, after all these years, it was a delight, following some false starts, to finally write a story about Laren Mapstone's past and how certain aspects of her character came to be. I had no idea back in the early '90s when I was drafting *Green Rider* that I would one day write a story about "T. Bankside" who had just been a name in a book. I knew nothing about him/her/them back then, and I'm pleased that this name evolved into an interesting and significant character in his own right. You just never know when you are writing a book what minor detail will develop into a larger story.

As for the acknowledgments, thank you as always to my superb book mom, Betsy Wollheim who loved *Green Rider* and opted for the right to publish it via her legendary company, DAW Books. Decades before *Green Rider* was a mote in my mind's eye, books published by DAW crowded out most others on my shelves. The quality of DAW's publications has not faltered thanks to the hard work of its editors and crew. I will note they've all been very patient with me.

My agent, Russ Galen, was there years before *Green Rider* was published. Even before he was my agent! I, a wannabe author, had sent him the manuscript (at his request via my query letter—you've got to do things the right way) and he turned it down. HOWEVER, he turned it down with a critique of what didn't work with that particular draft. The rejection letter did not upset me in the least or cause me to give up my dream of being published. In fact, it pumped me up. After all, it's not every day a topnotch literary agent will take time out of his busy schedule to offer a critique of one's manuscript. I received his rejection letter as a sign I was on the right track and got to work on a revision. The critique was super helpful in this endeavor.

When I resubmitted the manuscript, Russ' associate, Anna

Ghosh, offered to represent me. Eventually she moved on to found her agency and I became a part of Russ' amazing list of authors. It is he, as well, who encouraged me to try my hand at novellas, *et voila!*

I have to sneak in another thank you to a member of my literary agency, someone behind the scenes who probably is not often acknowledged in books: Denise De Mars-Vega. She is great with numbers and I am not, and I can't thank her enough for all her help.

Thank you also to my foreign rights agents, Danny Baror and Heather Baror-Shapiro. Without them, the series would not be seen outside of North America.

In my opinion, the cover art on this book by Donato Giancola is glorious. I love seeing a young Mapstone and the great oak with all the critters—SQUIRRELS! As I have stated more than once, I am fortunate in all my covers published by DAW and my overseas publishers. Since this is the 25th anniversary of *Green Rider,* I will mention in appreciation, the late master artist, Keith Parkinson, who painted the art for my first two books.

Thank you to my friend and copyeditor, Annaliese Jakimides, for her sensitive copyedit. She is a brilliant writer and artist herself, so it is an honor to have her fingerprints on my book.

You, the readers, have gotten me this far. Thank you so much. A book is never a book until it has readers. I am constantly astonished by how many of you appreciate the characters, world, and stories I've created. I am equally amazed and tickled by the community that has arisen around the books. Ride, Greenies, ride!

In that vein, I'd like to personally thank my Patreon patrons who have helped me over the past few years—you are awesome! They are: Mary Fye, Ana-Elizabeth Arnao, Kris, Glen Notman, Alyssa Jonas, Kathy Grant, Lyzz AnJo, Saralynn Brown, Candice Birdsong, Madbiologist, Emily Holum-Smith, Matt Weber, Anjali Jindal, Shakota Petrie, M. Kikstra, Hildie Johnson, Kyle Schwerdt, Natasha I. Mueller, Heather Robinson Lindsey, Steve Moody, Carna Steimel, Bethany Sheffer, Rebecca Elo, Teri Herbert, Lisa Wells, Tracy Frost, Catherine Kidd, Sherise Mitchell, Eve, Ted Hart, Wimelyn Santos, Tirzah Conway, Kelly Trahan, Pascal Doisteau Frérot, Rosie Brown, Laura Laubach-Richardson, Risa Kay, Jeremy Violette, Rosalie Boel, Meghan Notman, Jerri Stepp, Bethany McGee.

Thank you!

A WORD ABOUT THE INTERIOR ILLUSTRATIONS

For some reason, I decided to do illustrations for the interior pages of this novella. You would have thought I'd learned my lesson with the last one, *The Dream Gatherer*. Alas, no. I am not a professional, but I am, however, apparently a masochist.

All the illustrations, with the exception of the fern picture, were drawn with some form of ink, most of which was ballpoint pen. I like how you can vary the shading with a ballpoint pen. It's a little like using a pencil. Other types of pens/inks were used to help with highlighting, namely Pilot gel pens and Zebra felt tip paintbrush pens.

As for the fern picture . . . When it would not work for me with conventional pen and ink, I hopped onto ProCreate, which I'd never really used before, and decided to try creating it in pen and ink style with *stippling*. I don't know what I was thinking. (Did I mention I'm a masochist?) Perhaps I thought it was easier to erase than real ink. The ability to erase led to different problems, like erase and redo, erase and redo, erase and redo . . . I'll never be totally pleased with it. I may still be working on it to the end of my years. My hat is off to artists who can actually recreate the visions in their head on paper (or canvas, or screen, or?). I won't quit my day job.

ABOUT THE AUTHOR

Kristen Britain is the *New York Times* bestselling author of the Green Rider Series. She lives in the woods on an island in Maine and can be found online at kristenbritain.com.